Ema, the Captive

Conversations

Dinner

An Episode in the Life of a Landscape Painter

Ghosts

The Hare

How I Became a Nun

The Literary Conference

The Miracle Cures of Dr. Aira

The Musical Brain

The Seamstress and the Wind

Shantytown

Varamo

Ema, the Captive

•

CÉSAR AIRA

Translated by Chris Andrews

A NEW DIRECTIONS PAPERBOOK ORIGINAL

Originally published by Mondadori as *Ema, la cautiva* in 1997; published in conjunction with the Michael Gaeb Literary Agency / Berlin

Manufactured in the United States of America
First published as a New Directions Paperbook (NDP1364) in 2016
New Directions books are published on acid-free paper
Design by Erik Rieselbach

Library of Congress Cataloging-in-Publication Data
Names: Aira, César, 1949– author. | Andrews, Chris, 1962– translator.
Title: Ema, the captive / César Aira ; translated from the Spanish by Chris Andrews.
Other titles: Ema, la cautiva. English
Description: First American paperback edition. | New York : New Directions Publishing, 2016.
Identifiers: LCCN 2016009507 | ISBN 9780811219105 (alk. paper)
Subjects: LCSH: Single women—Argentina—Fiction. | Women prisoners—Fiction.
| Argentina—Social conditions—19th century—Fiction. | GSAFD: Historical fiction
Classification: LCC PQ7798.1.17 E4313 2016 | DDC 863/.64—dc23
LC record available at https://lccn.loc.gov/2016009507

10 9 8 7 6 5 4 3 2 1

New Directions Books are published for James Laughlin
by New Directions Publishing Corporation
80 Eighth Avenue, New York 10011

Contents

EMA, THE CAPTIVE   3

Author's note   231

EMA, THE CAPTIVE

A WAGON TRAIN WAS TRAVELING SLOWLY AT DAYBREAK; the soldiers leading the way swayed in the saddle half asleep, their mouths full of rancid saliva. With the change of season, they had been made to get up a few minutes earlier each day, so they went on sleeping as they rode, league after league, until the sun came up. The horses were spellbound or terrified by the mournful sound their hooves made on the plain, and by the contrast between the shadowy earth and the diaphanous depths of the air. The illumination of the sky seemed to be proceeding too quickly, without allowing night sufficient time to dissolve.

Unsheathed swords hung from the soldiers' belts. The cloth of their uniforms had been cut by clumsy hands, and the oversize kepis on their shaved heads made them look like boys. Those who were smoking were no more awake than the rest: lifting the cigarette and inhaling deeply were dream gestures. The smoke dissipated in the icy breeze. Birds scattered into the gray radiance, without making a sound. The prevailing silence was accentuated now and then by the distant cry of a lapwing, or the anxious, very high-pitched puffing of the horses; if not for the somnolence of their riders, they would have gone tearing off to their ruin, they were so spooked by the earth. But nothing emerged from those shadows, except, now and then, a weary hare running away through the grass, or a moth with six pairs of wings.

The oxen, by contrast — stumpy-legged creatures, which looked, in the halfslight, like caterpillars wriggling in a swamp — were completely mute; no one had ever heard them come out with so much as a murmur. There was only the sound of the water inside them, because they drank dozens of gallons a day; they were full, drunk on water. Four pairs pulled each of the wagons, which were as big as buildings. Their progress was so slow, and the amount of force required to move them so great, that they glided along with an imperturbable ease. The evenness of the terrain helped too, and above all the enormous diameter of the wheels, made of red wood, with a hollow metal globe at the hub, which was filled twice a day with honey-colored grease. The first wagons were covered and full of boxes, the rest were open and crowded with a motley throng, dozing or wearily shifting their chained limbs the better to stare at a blank and distant horizon.

But the sepia and bister light did not continue to brighten progressively. There came a moment when it began to fade, as if the day were yielding to an eternally impatient night; and soon, to complete the picture, it was raining darkly. The soldiers took the ponchos rolled up on their saddles and put them on, moving as listlessly as the indecisive rain that moistened their hands and released a penetrating odor from the horses' coats. The men and the women in the wagons did not move, except for one or two who raised their faces corpse-like to let the floating drizzle rinse them. Not one of them spoke. Some had not opened their eyes. Little by little the light returned and the clouds turned white. The lack of wind made the scene unreal.

After three or four hours, the rain stopped as it had begun, leaving the ground covered with reflections, transformed into another sky, no less terrifying for the fainthearted horses. At the tail end of the wagon train, a herd of two hundred grays straggled along: the reserves. They were very thin, with big expressive faces and heavy eyes. It had already been necessary to sacrifice many of the horses that had been ridden, and this would continue, so that all those in the rear guard would eventually be used. Dazed and barely able to see, the slightest stumble or the harmless bite of a toad was enough to put them out of action. In which case, of course, they were eaten: it was a kind of poetic justice.

So regular was the pampa's surface that, in the course of the whole morning, they encountered only one unevenness, which obliged them to deviate by no more than a few hundred yards from the straight line indicated by the guides: a set of deep ravines produced by some ancient geological disturbance, with walls of white and brown limestone, recently washed by the rain, in which the burrows of viscachas shone like onyx. Quivering bunches of dry jonquils hung over the edges, and a large rufous-collared sparrow shook the water from its feathers with vigorous wing-beats. Coming to the gullies, the soldiers seemed to emerge from their somnolence. One of them, a hirsute and scruffy man, went to the lieutenant and asked for permission to hunt viscachas for lunch. The officer merely shrugged his shoulders, making no effort to conceal how little he cared what they did or didn't do.

There were shouts, and ten soldiers broke away from the troop, heading for the ravines. The unexpectedness of the galloping threw the horses into a state of absolute terror; they flung their legs about randomly in a parody of a race, with their heads flailing and their vision obscured by bloody tears. Luckily for them, although they didn't know it, this kind of hunt was conducted on foot.

It was a lively and even colorful operation, given the relentless monotony of the background against which it unfolded. A man would put his face to the mouth of a burrow and yell out sharply. The viscachas, fast asleep at that time of day, would come rushing out without thinking, to be decapitated immediately. The men had to work with both hands (using a saber and a dagger that they called a *facón*) so abundant were the animals that sprang from the depths. They were harder to catch once they got out into the open or when two emerged at once; but in that case they were stabbed as they tried to climb up the cliffs, pinned against the soft limestone. The soldiers sweated as they ran around slashing at the big white rodents, many of which came out carrying their young, which remained beside the decapitated bodies of their mothers, lapping up the blood. The men were pleased to see that they were plump, in fine condition. The biggest were three feet long, and when one slipped

away and ran among the legs of the horses, which were un-
nerved already by the powerful stench of blood, havoc broke
loose. The countless dogs that were following the wagons
ran to the gully, barking like demons. They dared to bite only
the wounded viscachas, and more than one was accidentally
slashed by a saber or deliberately beaten to a pulp if it tried
to steal from the catch. It was miraculous that the dogs had
survived, since they were never fed, and even more miraculous that they had persisted in the journey. Once the last viscacha was laid out between the stream and the puddles of blood,
the men tied them into bunches by their tails; but before getting back onto their horses, they went looking for the young,
no bigger than a fist at that time of year. They used the tips of
their knives to open a hole in the stomach of the live animal, to
which they applied their lips. With a single suck they ingested
the soft, warm insides, all blood and milk. They threw the little
empty bags that were left to the dogs, who had to make do with
that, and the odd severed head.

Meanwhile, the wagon train had moved on, and was now a
couple of leagues ahead. After midday it began to drizzle again,
and the lieutenant gave the order to halt for lunch.

Beside the wagons, the soldiers constructed hemispheres
of tarred paper to protect the fires. Under the disdainful gaze
of the convicts, they busied themselves skinning the viscachas
with fabulous skill, then skewering them on iron spits and
scorching them over the fire for a few minutes; their flesh was
pure white, like that of a sole, but tasted sour.

On this journey, prisoners and soldiers lived on the same diet of jerky and biscuits, except that the prisoners were given half rations. They had no reason to lament this, since they expended no energy at all, and passed the time sleeping, propped against one another in the wagons. As for the officers, they regularly accompanied (or replaced) this standard fare with brandy. Their alimentary routine was modified only when they came across a flock of rheas or partridges, or flushed out a quail or a hare, whose flight the lieutenant would take pleasure in stopping with a well-aimed shot.

While the maté water was coming to the boil, three adjutants cut the jerky into strips and proceeded to hand it out, working their way along the train. The effort of eating was repugnant to the prisoners, such was their state of weakness and torpor; some of them had to be punched to make them reach out and take the biscuit and the mug, into which another soldier aimed a boiling jet of the green liquid.

The four officers sat down on the high-backed saddles that they had carelessly flung to the ground. Indifferent to the rain, they stared off into the void, their gazes hovering somewhere between stupidity and malice. For months now they had been ignoring the silent multitude in their charge; they felt like free planets spinning at random in a limbo of alcohol and vacant time. There were ten corporals, but they were often stripped of their rank, sometimes for no apparent reason, and in any case they blended into the rank and file, among whom there was nothing remotely resembling military discipline. Except in the lieutenant's presence, no one respected the conventions, and even he considered them frivolous and archaic. These were savage men, becoming more savage as they marched southward. In the desert, a space outside the rule of law in nineteenth-century Argentina, reason was deserting them as well.

The lieutenant, supreme and sole authority over the wagon train, was a young man—he looked about thirty-five—who had been living on the frontier for at least ten years. He had undertaken a number of these journeys, transporting human cargo from Buenos Aires, each of which had taken almost a year, there and back. He had white, soft hands (he removed his gloves only at night), black, oiled hair, and when he walked he wobbled in an awkward, ungainly fashion because of the width of his hips, which were out of proportion with his skinny arms and legs. By contrast, he was an excellent horseman, the only one who used an English saddle with a pommel.

The major under his command was an old man with long gray hair and a tattered uniform; the other two officers were taciturn sergeants with Indian features. The lieutenant unscrewed the cap of his canteen and took a swig of brandy. The others imitated him mechanically. Drinking was second nature to them. The rain continued, imperceptibly fine. Thunderclaps resounded from the dark horizon. The lieutenant took his watch from his pocket and stared at it as if in a stupor: two o'clock.

Finally the adjutant brought them the roasted viscacha and a bag of biscuits. They didn't eat as much as they drank, and throughout the whole lunch not a word was spoken. The lieutenant didn't taste the food; he failed to react when they offered him a piece, and went on smoking. Carelessly, he let the rain extinguish and ruin his cigarette. He threw it away and rolled another, but took no more care to protect it. He drank continually, emptying his canteen, which had been refilled twice in the course of the morning. Now he ordered one of the sergeants to fill it up again, and when it was returned to him he took a long swig. His attitude was coherent, at least.

"And the Frenchman?" he suddenly asked in a murky voice. The words stood out beautifully against the ambient strangeness. The men were slow to take in the question; first they had to look at the wet grass and the blue bones of the viscacha; one fixed his gaze on the lieutenant's muddy boots. Then they looked around. The line of still wagons stretched away for hundreds of yards, and everything was silent and mired movement.

"He'll be over there," ventured the major pointing with his beard at the sleeping huddle of horses. He too was surprised by the sound of his own voice.

He sent for the Frenchman, although it seemed a waste of time. They found him beside one of the horses, trying to make a saddle blanket with viscacha skins. Since they hadn't been tanned, within a few days they would start to give off an unbearable stench, and permanently foul the saddle, and infect the horse, but he didn't know that.

He tried to explain to the sergeant that he wasn't hungry, but followed him after hesitating briefly, supposing that the lieutenant might have something to say to him. He didn't want to slight the others, although the idea of having to join them was abhorrent. He found the lunch stops unspeakably dreary, and the rain made today's almost unbearable.

All the lieutenant did was invite him to taste the game. The Frenchman repressed a sigh of discontent. With two fingers he picked up a snow-white thigh, wet with rain, and took a bite. It wasn't as bad as he had expected. The taste was reminiscent of deer and of pheasant. Trying to ignore the lifeless gazes fixed on him, he went on eating and, with an occasional swig of brandy, got through a whole quarter.

But before ten minutes had gone by, he threw it all up spectacularly, seized by the most dreadful dizziness. He had gone completely white. When there was nothing left in his stomach, he walked for a while with his eyes shut and then tried to eat a hard biscuit, also wet with rain, chewing conscientiously. But even that made him feel nauseous, so he gave up.

He was an engineer who had been hired by the central government to undertake special projects on the frontier. A few days after getting off the ship, he had attached himself to a contingent of convicts that happened to be leaving for his destination. Given his sudden transplantation, he was bound to be disconcerted by the unreal conditions of the desert. He didn't speak the language or understand it. To him, the men were animals and their company inhuman. He was small and delicate, about thirty-five years old, with an overly voluminous head and a large Assyrian beard in the style of the day. He had a blue suit and a gray one, which he wore on alternate days, always with the jacket buttoned up to the neck. Exposure to the elements had turned his face and hands red, and the visions afforded by the journey had left a puzzled gleam in his blue eyes. He used spectacles of green glass against the barbaric glare of the plains, in spite of which his eyes watered constantly. The cape he had put on that morning to protect him from rain was so heavy it made him sweat; he kept having to mop his face with a handkerchief and discreetly wring out his beard.

When he felt that he had recovered sufficient self-control to speak, he addressed the lieutenant.

"I suppose it was a mistake, trying to eat that animal."

"I suppose so," replied the lieutenant sarcastically.

"It didn't agree with me at all."

"I noticed. The soldiers eat the young raw."

Duval could not help grimacing in disgust, which drew a contemptuous laugh from his interlocutor.

"You'll have to make do with partridges and *aguapampa*."

The mention of partridges depressed the engineer. Of all the foods provided by the pampa and the army supplies, those little birds were the only thing his stomach could tolerate, as long as they were properly roasted, but since he completely lacked the skills required to catch them, he had to depend on the whims of the gauchos, who would sometimes let a big flock go by indifferently, regarding them as inferior fare; they were even less excited by the work of plucking them, of course. So Duval often had to subsist for a week or more on biscuits (the mere smell of the dried meat disgusted him) and the awful boiled maté that gave him stomach cramps and provoked a constant, unbearable need to urinate.

He had sat down next to the lieutenant, whom he disliked intensely; but there was no one else with whom he could speak French, and he was still a long way from being able to keep up a conversation in Spanish. Indeed, he was less and less confident that he would be able to master the language, with so few opportunities to learn it, surrounded as he was by brutes who spoke in grunts; he knew that on the frontier a half-Indian dialect was used, so he would have to start all over again.

After a moment, however, the lieutenant smiled somewhat less maliciously and, with calculated indifference, startled Duval with this disclosure:

"We'll be reaching Azul tonight. You'll be able to feast yourself."

"What? Tonight?" stammered the Frenchman, painfully aware once again of his ignorance concerning the length and duration of the journey. The fort at Azul was the last stopping-place on the way, and although he'd been looking forward to getting there for weeks, he hadn't realized how close it was. He tried to control his excitement by rubbing his hands. The other officers were still daydreaming, as if words spoken in another language were inaudible to them. Duval waited for further information, but none was forthcoming.

"What time will we arrive?"

The lieutenant merely shrugged and spat. He produced a

case containing slender cigars and invited the Frenchman to take one, without looking him in the eye (he never did). Peering through the smoke as it dispersed in the drizzle, Duval observed him with a genuine curiosity. Before the beginning of the journey, he had been told that Lieutenant Lavalle came from a very wealthy landed family, and had been educated in French and English schools. That information had not prepared him for a man who had given himself with such ardor to savagery in all its countless forms—quite the opposite. Lavalle's clear delight in barbarity exceeded that of the most primitive soldiers, and perhaps even the prisoners, who were no longer human. From the start, Duval had noticed a morbid disorder of the soul in his total indifference to nature: he couldn't tell one bird from another, or a mouse from a hare, or clover from verbena. It was a blindness seasoned with insanity, a kind of obsession in reverse, which sometimes filled his unwilling companion with horror. Although it was also possible that his erroneous answers were simply another manifestation of his twisted sense of humour.

Duval went on smoking and drinking, and paid the lieutenant no more heed. The gray sky had turned white, and over the horizon the atmosphere was hatched with oblique stripes of yellow sunlight and blue rain. The soldiers drowsed, their bellies full. Duval went for a walk along the row of wagons, trying to overcome the weakness he felt after vomiting. He made himself walk as much as he could every time they stopped, even though his weariness had grown with the passing days and finally soaked into every bone in his body. Only by walking could he dispel the melancholy caused by continual contact with the horses, which were so different from those he had ridden in Europe that at times he could hardly believe they belonged to the same species. The creole breed was a contradiction, a blemish on the animal kingdom, and of the many surprises afforded by the journey, those creatures were the greatest. He had changed horses three times already, replacing them as they died (one had expired under him, startled by a tiny dancing moth) with others that were no less fainthearted: distorted masses of viscera, skin and dry hair, held together by fear alone. Now he walked as far away from the horses as he could, staring at his boots and the clumps of grass. The oxen he found more bearable, although they were monstrous too: excessively cylindrical, with their little snake-like heads.

He would, of course, have been happy to endure these eccentricities of the New World had he found himself in less disturbing company ... He threw a sidelong glance at the prisoners, wondering how they could bear the immobility. The mere thought of it was enough to make him stagger. For barely half an hour, at dusk and under the strictest supervision, they were unchained and allowed to get out of the wagons, but most of them preferred to stay where they were. It was surprising that they had survived so many weeks of vegetable stillness, packed in together and barely fed. He wondered how the army could justify the expense of transporting them to the forts, since they were barely alive by this stage. But of course he had no idea

what went on there at the edge of the world. And those un-
fortunates may have been hardier than their conditions would
have lead one to presume; according to the lieutenant, they often rioted, and that was why they were subjected to a control
that never relented, not for one minute, and grew in severity as
the train pursued its journey into the province.

Duval never went near the wagons, and the stench they
were giving off that day was unbearable, as if the rain had released the most revolting effluvia from the tortured bodies of
the prisoners and the depths of their changeless bedding—in
spite of which they were sleeping or staring impassively into
space. Suddenly a woman's hoarse voice asked him for a cigarette. Startled, Duval pretended not to hear her and, in his confusion, threw the cigarette he was smoking into a puddle. At
night, the officers would take some of the women and ride away
with them. At the first stream they crossed after leaving Buenos Aires, they had made the prisoners wash and cropped their
hair, but hygienic measures after that had been rudimentary.
Duval, of course, had abstained from all contact. In the wagons,
promiscuity reigned, and seemed, like so many other things
on this journey, to waver between the permissible and the pro-
hibited. The elusiveness of the laws in force had been demon-
strated in a particularly brutal way not long before. In one of the
wagons, a man was copulating noisily with a being of indefinite
sex, in broad daylight, without hiding. This was not an exceptional sight, and no more offensive than many others; it was
merely surprising that any of them still had the energy. Duval,

who was riding nearby, didn't even avert his gaze. He was about to spur his horse along when he saw the swollen, livid face of the lieutenant, passing him and heading for the wagon. Lavalle was clearly having a bad day, and yet he acted with an apathetic indifference, just as his victim would have, given the opportunity. Leaning to one side of his English saddle, he grabbed the man by the hair, and, with a single jerk, detached him from his companion and threw him out of the wagon. The man was left hanging head down from the chain attached to his bony ankle. Duval, who had thought that the punishment would end there, watched in astonishment as the lieutenant severed his genitals with a slash of his saber, and the man passed out, bathed in his own blood. He remained in that position until he died, and it was only three days later, when the stench of the corpse was making the air unbreathable all along the wagon train, that Lavalle consented to getting rid of the body.

The sun was already setting when one of the guides who was riding ahead lifted his hand to signal the first glimpse of Azul and the surrounding settlements in the distance. Duval, possessed by a weariness that had grown too large for his physical body to contain, was improvising a ballad to the rhythm of his horse, a ballad about the dusk, repeating words in his melodious native tongue and thinking (as he had thought every day at that hour for more than a month now) that a novel could be written about those changes of color in the sky and the transformations of the clouds between say, six and eight, so long as the author confined himself to the most rigorous realism. The resulting novel, a report on atmospheric colors, shifts, and flows, would be the apotheosis of life's futility. Why not? A supremely stupid saga; the world was ripe for such a work, or would be by the time he finished writing it. Every evening he observed that clichéd daily chaos with passionate attention, and dreamed. An avid reader of novels since childhood, his favorites had been adventures in wild, exotic locations, and now that he found himself in such a setting, he realized that what counts in the unfolding of an adventure is how the days repeat one another exactly. "Adventures," he said to himself, "are always adventures in boredom."

Although Duval's eyesight was good, he was the only one who couldn't see; the others were pointing directly at the setting sun, and it was dazzling him. But a couple of hours later, when the lieutenant gave the order to halt, Duval could make out rows of huts distributed over an area that seemed limitless. He inquired about the strange form looming on the horizon.

The lieutenant replied that it was the fort.

"But it must be enormous!"

"Not really. You lose your sense of proportion out here."

And thereupon he invited the Frenchman to dine with him in Azul. Although surprised by the sudden courtesy, Duval accepted with pleasure and waited while the lieutenant organized the setting up of the camp and the roster of sentries, duties that he discharged with an obvious aversion. Then they set off at a gallop, just the two of them, in the last of the daylight.

Azul, at that time, was what might be called a typical desert settlement: no more than four hundred white inhabitants, almost all of them huddled together in a palatial fort, and somewhere between five and six thousand "tame Indians," who did everything, while the masters tended their idleness, dreaming of economic or military exploits. The Indian tents were scattered between the tributaries of a gray river that flowed sluggishly to the south, from which the white people refused to drink because, they said, its water had a brackish aftertaste; so they used wine and liquor to quench their thirst, with predictable results. The fort rose up in the middle of the settlement: originally a square stockade with watchtowers at the corners, it had expanded disproportionately in all directions because of the swelling population within. It had come to resemble a Tower of Babel, or rather a motley toy city, with tiny huts clinging to the walls, chaotic hives of rooms piled one on top of another, bridges and suspended passageways with children running across them, and women hanging washing from precarious lines.

When he was able to take his eyes off this fantastic construction, Duval realized that he was passing through the suburbs where the savages lived; many were sitting peacefully on the ground with cigarettes between their fingers, showing absolutely no interest in the strangers. It was the first time he had seen Indians, and he would have liked to examine them more closely, but the lieutenant was rushing on, and he didn't want to be left behind.

The fort did not have gates. They proceeded at a walking pace through a maze of shacks until they reached the headquarters, an imposing stone edifice with two asymmetrical wings. An Indian stationed at the door took charge of their horses and clearly found them amusing. Lavalle brushed the dust from his uniform and removed his gloves. Haughtily, he ordered a subaltern to announce his presence to the colonel. After the formalities, a lieutenant led them down long corridors to an anteroom plunged in almost total darkness, where he left them for a minute.

In the commander's office, two pink crystal oil lamps lit up the heavy mahogany and bronze furniture. Colonel Leal was a small and distinguished-looking old man, with white hair and a sad, kind face. He embraced the lieutenant, who called him "uncle," and turned ceremoniously toward Duval, with whom, once introduced, he began to speak in fluent French, without an accent.

"I'm absolutely delighted by your visit. I have so few opportunities to practise my French here ..."

"It's perfect, I can assure you. Have you lived in France?"

"I spent long years in your dear country, before the accession of the tyrant, of course."

It took Duval a moment to realize that he meant Bonaparte. Treading warily, he changed the subject.

"But here, the language ..."

"Quite, my dear friend. No one speaks the sweet tongue of Ronsard on the pampa. Why should they? I can't think of a single valid reason. Sometimes I'm surprised not to have forgotten it myself. If not for my books ... And a few of my officers who, luckily, are educated ... But you'll find out for yourself! There won't be many people you can talk to there in Pringles, and my colleague Espina certainly won't be one of them," he concluded, laughing.

Espina was the commander of the fort in Pringles. The rumors about him were most alarming and had become a source of grave preoccupation for Duval, who would be under the man's orders, and his alone, once he reached the frontier. Espina was said to be a semi-savage, with Indian blood in his veins, excited by horrors and tyrannical in the extreme.

The colonel poured out three glasses of cognac and chatted animatedly for a while with his nephew. Duval, sunk in a large armchair, drowsed in a haze of fatigue and lethargy. Asked if he would like to take a bath before dinner, he replied with an almost incredulous yes. It seemed absurd: the civilized world had become an illusion; but the colonel rang a little bell, and ordered an aide to take Duval to one of the guest rooms and prepare the bath for him. The engineer followed the servant like a puppet. He smoked while he waited, then took off his clothes and lowered himself into the water with a rictus of pleasure that was almost painful. Half an hour later he was drying himself with a large white towel. Before dressing he powdered and perfumed himself, using the flasks on the dresser. He noticed with some surprise that the pink wallpaper was only one of many feminine touches: perhaps it had been the room of a mistress. He threw himself onto the bed and dozed for a while until the same servant came to take him to the dining room.

At dinner, with the commander, Lieutenant Lavalle, and two other officers, the conversation was conducted entirely in French. The barefoot servants attending them had to constantly replace the bottles of champagne, which emptied themselves as if by magic. Each time they came in or went out, the candlelight flickered, setting off delicious verbal scintillations in the mind of the Frenchman, who after an initial moment of anxiety, discovered that he was indeed able to eat and drink abundantly, and proceeded to do so without a moment's respite. He enjoyed the evening, although he was melancholically aware that the brilliance of the conversation and the consummate skill with which his companions obliged him to assume the metropolitan's disdainful superiority were mirages that would vanish in the blink of an eye. After all, he said to himself, good manners are an illusion, transparent as the air, and these dreadful, contradictory gentlemen exist merely to represent the inoffensive emptiness of strategy. Lieutenant Lavalle was carving a duck with silver instruments; from time to time he threw Duval a glance that was difficult to interpret.

The Frenchman's gastronomical misadventures during the voyage, related in detail by the lieutenant, were a source of great amusement. Duval burst out laughing too and, as he polished off a dozen oysters, wondered if it hadn't all been a dream. The story of the viscacha, still fresh in memory, made the colonel laugh until he cried.

"I too once tried to eat one of those filthy rodents," he said. "With the same result."

They spoke of the natives and their food.

"With the animals they hunt," said one of the local officers, "the Indians prepare more sophisticated meals than you might expect, given their poverty. But it's hard for a white men to get used to that food, and if he does, he tends to lose his taste for conventional fare."

"No great loss," said Lavalle.

His uncle contradicted him: "It could be a source of endless melancholy."

He spoke as if from personal experience. There was something quite mysterious about the colonel. Duval wondered what curious fortuity had brought these refined bon vivants to the desert. After a while, the conversation returned to matters of more immediate concern. The lieutenant, who had been away from Pringles for almost a year, asked for news of the town, but the others could tell him very little. Although they had all been there at least once, the officers in Azul regarded Pringles as remote and inaccessible, almost like Indian territory. Besides, they were busy enough with their own problems: two months earlier, Azul had received the unexpected visit of a raiding party ... Startled, Duval listened attentively. There had been ten thousand Indians, in a lightning attack; they came at night on their fastest horses, rustled all the cattle, leaving a thousand cut throats behind and almost all the soldiers without wives. For weeks the settlers had been forced to live on game and fish; the flocks were just being replenished.

"Which tribe were they from?" asked Lavalle.

"We don't know. You should have seen them: painted, with their feathers ... Quite a show. They seemed to have come a long way. Our 'tame' Indians said they were Catriel's warriors, but that's very doubtful."

Colonel Leal said that right after the attack he had sent a detachment to Pringles, thinking that it might have been laid waste, because it was on the route the raiding party must have taken. But no. They hadn't seen the columns of warriors, and they didn't even let the detachment spend the night in the fort. Needless to say, Leal's officers were not granted an audience with Espina.

"As you see," he concluded, "the stronghold remains impenetrable. Sometimes I wonder if we wouldn't do better to simply forget that it exists."

"Something just occurred to me," said Lavalle. "Could it be that Espina has negotiated a separate peace agreement with Catriel?"

Leal laughed noisily.

"No, absolutely not! None of the important chiefs, and Catriel least of all, would bother doing that. In fact I don't think the Indians even know there's a fort there, because it's hidden by the very forest whose limits it's supposed to secure. When they set off on a military expedition, the savages come out onto the pampa leagues and leagues before getting to Pringles, to save time."

He turned to Duval and proceeded to give him a supplementary explanation:

"The idea of establishing *two* lines of forts, dreamed up by the incompetent Alsina, was hopelessly premature and over-ambitious; it merely created a no-man's-land that's impossible to guard, where the hordes can roam about as they like. The new line, with Pringles as its central point, was supposed to render our defensive forces obsolete, and allow settlers to take up land. But no: the attacks keep coming just as often and un-expectedly, while Pringles is ever more distant, like a planet drifting out of our gravitational field."

He took a gulp of champagne before continuing: "In fact, given the adverse conditions, the fort should have failed, and would have, if not for Espina. Without him, Pringles would vanish in a moment. In that deranged environment, his defects have turned out to be virtues: his wildness and savagery have preserved him from the violent death he no doubt deserves. He's also notoriously stingy, which stimulates his initiative. He has done deals with certain tribes, and maintains a very brisk trade with them; we once received, for example, some pieces of the Indians' famous white pottery. Not only that: he prints money, like the caudillos in Entre Rios ... He can get away with anything because of his miraculous capacity to survive, though it's not at all clear that his survival is of any use to us, as the raid-ers showed when they came to visit a few days ago."

The image that Duval was forming of this character was laden with dark overtones. He was wondering what it would be like to work for such a man: all-powerful, beyond the law. He didn't even know what his work would consist of, since he was to receive his instructions *in situ* from the outlandish colonel himself.

"And what do you know about living conditions there?" asked the lieutenant. "Have there been famines?"

"In Pringles? I don't think so!" The colonel laughed. "Quite the opposite! Although I barely know him, I can assure you that Espina would go without anything rather than food. I suppose he needs it to keep moving, as a crocodile needs its siestas in the mud. And with the forest so close at hand, he has an unlimited supply of large and small game; all he has to do (and he's had plenty of time) is find one of those valleys full of jaguars and deer. Whether or not the Indians let him intrude on their preserve is another matter. But Espina is very resourceful. He belongs to that caste of prosperous barbarians with a gift for handling reversals of fortune; they always come out on top, although they're magnets for adversity. A few years ago," Leal continued, still addressing himself to the Frenchman, "shortly after the foundation of the fort, there were rumors of cannibalism, false of course, the sort that often circulate in circumstances like that; indeed it might be said that no foundation is complete without such a myth. I once sent the colonel a cutting from the Las Flores newspaper, with a caricature of him as Nebuchadnezzar eating grass ... But don't be alarmed, you'll soon be able to see for yourself that it's all a fabrication; these days, I imagine, Espina prefers the charatas he buys from the Indians, stuffed with truffles and plums by his cooks."

"Isn't trade with the Indians forbidden?"

"The arm of the law is not that long. Whatever happens from here on," the colonel said, gesturing to indicate the land to the west, "is beyond the control of any authority or legislation. But you know, oddly, I don't think Espina's trading contravenes any order, since he's using money that he prints himself; so from the central government's point of view those deals simply don't exist."

The servants refilled the glasses, allowing Duval to drown his astonishment. The colonel changed the subject: "I don't envy those poor wretches you're taking to Pringles," he said with a sigh. He was speaking to the Frenchman. "If you thought the conditions they traveled in were bad, wait till you see what the poor devils will have to bear, men and women alike ... Except the women attractive enough to be chosen for the harem ..."

He looked inquiringly at Lavalle, who shook his head: "Forget it. She would have been sold to a rancher in Buenos Aires. These women are for the troops, although they're so battered and burdened with children, I suspect not even the soldiers will deign to accept them."

"In that case ... They won't survive for long. Since the fort was built, ten years ago, the convoys of prisoners have kept coming, one a year, with more than a thousand convicts each time, and the white population of Pringles today is no more than three hundred! Of course we are speaking of individuals cast out by society once and for all ... But why condemn them to such short and unproductive lives, when it would be simpler to have them work as laborers or servants? Another of our stupid government's many whims. You haven't noticed any signs of change?" he asked his nephew, whom he knew to be on good terms with certain people who worked for the Chief of Staff.

"Not in the least. In fact, I think the opposite opinion prevails. I wouldn't be surprised if they began to use banishment to punish even less serious crimes."

"Is there much desertion?" Duval asked.

The colonel chose to answer metaphorically: "Beyond a certain limit (I'm afraid you'll have to get used to this: we're always speaking of limits and frontiers here) everything is desertion, since no one is in the right place."

After the chocolate rolls with ice cream, they got up and went to the colonel's library for coffee. He had chosen to entertain them in his private quarters because Lavalle was a relative and in deference to the foreign guest. The bound volumes covering the walls, a few old oil paintings of hunting scenes, the leather armchairs and the dim light created the anomalous atmosphere of an English club. The strong, aromatic coffee was ready, but Duval was not surprised to see that they all preferred to keep refilling their brandy glasses.

The colonel invited him to take a seat beside his own.

"Perhaps we have frightened you a little with our chatter," he said confidentially. "But pay no attention. We get bored and pass the time gossiping, so I dare say our stories were rather tall. In Pringles, despite everything, you will find some of the comforts that make for an agreeable life. It's such a decadent place ... You'll be able to have as many servants as you please and, whatever the nature of your work, you'll have a great deal of free time." His face took on a dreamy look. "And I assure you that leisure in Pringles is something to savor. Eight years have passed already since I was there for the first and last time, and I still remember it: the forest, El Pillahuinco, is a paradise ... I don't believe there's a region in the world to match its beauty. *Là, tout n'est qu'ordre et beauté, luxe, calme et volupté,*" he concluded, tracing an arc with his cigar.

The young engineer did not reply, nor did he know what to think. When he retired, before midnight, he found that his bed had been made with silk sheets. He found it difficult to go to sleep under a roof, in a bed, and he woke up with the first light of dawn, although there was not a sound to be heard.

They spent the following day and night in Azul, taking on provisions for the remaining thirty days of the journey. The troops were camped a league from the fort, and from morning to night, curious locals ventured out on horseback or in buggies to set eyes on the terrible prisoners bound for the frontier. But the actual sight of those remnants was disappointing: months in chains had reduced them to skin and bone.

The Frenchman had lunch with the colonel, just the two of them this time, except for the deathly soldiers who, with pale and brittle hands, served them crumbly woodcocks and mashed potatoes. Above the colonel's tiny bald spot, two identical scenes carved in the wood paneling caught Duval's eye, but discerning what they represented was beyond his powers of concentration. The soldiers wheeled in a mahogany mixing bowl, from which they served the ice cream with a silver spoon. The end of the meal went on for hours, the old man talking nonstop in his antiquated French, downing glass after glass. Eventually, having emptied six bottles of champagne and one of brandy, and tossed the corks for the colonel's cat to chase, they fell asleep in armchairs in the study. When they woke, the colonel asked his guest if he would be interested in a tour of the settlement, to which Duval replied that what he would most enjoy would be to meet the Indians.

Leal's cheeks contracted in a vague smile.

"You're bound to see them, there are so many. But don't get your hopes up; they're fundamentally dull."

"I thought they would surprise me."

"Quite the contrary."

The colonel sent for a lieutenant who spoke French and introduced him to Duval. The lieutenant was a young man, barely out of boyhood, with blond hair, translucent skin and feminine features. The Frenchman guessed that he must be another scion of the plutocracy sent to the provinces to complete his education. He was loquaciously timid.

"Machines or Indians," was the choice he proposed.

"Indians, of course," replied the engineer. "Pistons and pulleys are dead as dinosaurs. I want to see my savage brothers."

The young man laughed.

"They're not savage any more, regrettably," he said.

They went to the Indian camp, riding little silky white mares. The dwellings, scattered over a great expanse, all a long way apart, reared in the pallid air. Didn't the dispersion make them more vulnerable to attacks? True, the lieutenant admitted, but that was of no consequence at all. The tents were too small, life too vast. Had they all been reflected on a needle-point, they would still have been out of place in the landscape. Was there some order to their disposition? The lieutenant said no, but the Frenchman, whose eye was topographically trained, thought he could distinguish a double arc, albeit irregular, which his guide dismissed as an illusion, pointing out that every time there was a raid, the Indians took refuge in the fort and their dwellings were razed. When they came out again, they rebuilt them haphazardly.

"But that's what I was referring to, that randomness," said the Frenchman.

"They put them up anywhere."

"Palaces have been built in random places too."

He was distracted by the unusual quantity of dogs, and by their curious appearance: small, like dwarf greyhounds, with pointed muzzles (which might have indicated a change in their feeding habits, following the extinction of American mice), light gray in color, and totally mute.

"How do they feed them?" asked Duval.

"They're as frugal as angels," replied the lieutenant. "An insect, a blade of grass, that's all they need."

He caught one so that Duval could feel its weight: a quarter pound at most, maybe less, the Frenchman reckoned, stroking the animal. They could not have moved had they been any heavier, for there was almost no strength in their muscles, and their bite, as Duval was encouraged to discover for himself, was as harmless as the suction of a butterfly.

Equally striking were the numerous children running around everywhere in big shrieking bands or dragging complicated paper toys: they were uniformly thin, with prominent abdomens and straight black hair. Their voices had a delicate timbre and always sounded distant.

"All the women do is procreate," said the lieutenant, indirectly explaining the acoustic effect. "If it's not their husbands getting them pregnant, it's the soldiers, who are always coming to visit. The flow of births is steady, continuous, and unlimited, and it raises questions that remain unresolved, since the communism of the Indians makes it impossible to group them into families. Strange, isn't it? So far, no one has come up with a way to exploit the situation."

"Exploit?"

There was no reply. Duval felt a shiver run down his spine as he tried to imagine the kind of schemes an imaginative adolescent might hatch on that virgin yet extraordinarily populated frontier. The mechanisms of prehistory are too hard to leave behind, he thought. Perhaps he should have gone to see the machines instead.

Suddenly he realized that his young host had no secrets: he was laying his whole being bare to the casual observer, and the most inflexible necessity ordained that it should be so. Duval could travel all over the world, it would always be the same: human beings were devoid of mystery. It was something they had never possessed: that was what made them human. When this revelation came to him, at that precise moment in his life, Duval felt a great liberating surprise. He was surprised to discover that there was no need to go to Laputa or Pringles in search of oracles. What an utter waste of time!

Dinner was copious, and this time it was served in the fort's main dining room, with all the officers in attendance, wearing dress uniforms and white gloves. Indian musicians played; there was a long drinking session. Since the colonel liked to sleep in, and they would be leaving at dawn, they took their leave that evening, Lavalle for a few months, since he regularly traveled to the capital with dispatches, the engineer for a year, the duration of his contract.

"We'll see each other again in twelve months' time, then," said Colonel Leal, and added: "It will be an unforgettable experience, from which you're well equipped, I'm sure, to draw the most valuable lessons."

The next morning, after a few hours' march, Azul disappeared from view, and once again they found themselves in the solitude of the pampa, which was even flatter and emptier than before. The only relief from that vastness was provided by enormous ombú trees, which appeared every two or three days, always in isolation. The ombús were curious plants, deformed by the atmosphere, similar to baobabs, though not nearly as tall, with big weary branches resting on the earth and poisonous leaves of a green so dark it was almost black.

The absolute monotony of the journey continued, except

that the night watch had to be reinforced because they were now in Indian territory. On the clearest days they could make out the blue line of the mountains on the horizon, and from time to time they thought they could see horsemen in the shimmering distance, but under scrutiny the figures vanished. One afternoon a stronger breeze than usual began to blow (there were no real winds in the region, Duval was told), and since it was coming from the west, it brought a vague scent of vegetation, which the soldiers claimed to recognize as the smell of El Pillahuinco. The Frenchman filled his lungs, trying to absorb the emanations. He breathed and breathed, methodically, telling himself that otherwise he would die of boredom.

Spring advanced little by little. Sometimes their route took them across vast carpets of tiny red and yellow flowers, covered with bees; sometimes they marched for leagues through fields of camomile, which released an intoxicating odor when crushed, or over little violets, so numerous they turned the plain blue and hid the earth. The grasses were no more than five or six inches tall; only the odd lonely thistle rose higher, its lilac tuft impregnated with pollen, which stained the lazy horseflies.

Rain fell without interruption, day and night, heralding the warm season: it was never heavy, usually no more than a delicate drizzle suspended in the air, without consistency or direction, and hardly noticeable in the end, so used to it had they become. Birds returning from the west passed overhead, always flying singly, very high, flapping silently through the moist air, like fish. Marching over the dwarf chañar trees, the travelers felt like giants treading a miniature forest, which reproduced a real one in every detail. There was a kind of natural bonsai called *alpataco*, a foot tall.

Every day, whenever the sun was able to slip a ray through a gap in the clouds, they were treated to the spectacle of a rainbow. They never knew where it would appear: sometimes so close that it seemed the slow wagons were about to pass under it; sometimes very far away, fine and fragile as a crystal.

The earth had turned to mud; it made a sensual squelching sound under the animals' hooves. A profusion of insects emerged interminably from the wet ground: big mosquitos hopping like locusts; spiders spinning dome-shaped webs; pretty green bugs the size and shape of coins, with arabesques that were always different (Duval began a collection, not out of scientific curiosity but for the simple childish pleasure of laying out his specimens on a blanket when the caravan stopped for the night, and arranging them in rows). Above all, there were the grotesque dragonflies with their bulging eyes, which could be popped out with a little squeeze to lie in the palm of the hand like two tiny red balls. They also saw a curious insect, a kind of mantis, which the gauchos called a *tata-dios*. It was as big as a dove, and had so many joints that its definitive form remained elusive: there was always something more to unfold.

In quantity and effect, however, nothing could match the toads that had appeared from nowhere, mostly as small as partridge eggs but occasionally enormous and disproportionate—there was no in-between. As the horses approached, the toads moved out of the way (those little hops were soon very familiar): beautiful creatures, in shades of bluish to yellowish green, with elaborate, shiny scales on their backs, gobbling insects with an insatiable voracity. Duval was fascinated by their feeding as much as by their sheer abundance. Sometimes, to pass the time, he would try to calculate how many toads there must be in the country's millions of acres of virgin land. He would multiply the number in a square yard (a hundred) by ten thousand, then multiply that product by a hundred, then by a thousand, then by a hundred million, and even then he knew that he wasn't close to the total. He amused himself by comparing this quantity with the number of minutes or seconds in a year or a human life, letting his imagination roam among the awe-inspiring multiplications accomplished by those useless creatures. And as he proceeded through that sea of little green jewels, which leaped or froze, hypnotized by the sun, he felt a strange exaltation swelling his breast.

"The species is everything," he thought, "the individual doesn't count; man disappears into the world..."

What would have disturbed others filled him with an inexplicable delight: he was anticipating pleasures that he had not yet even dreamed of, and with each step he took toward the wild and mysterious west, he felt that he was entering the sacred realm of impunity, that is, of human freedom, the exercise of which was something that he had not been taught in the old world and would have to learn in the forests of America, at the cost of his own dissolution.

Like another part of the same idea, there was the muteness of the animals, which was in keeping with everything else: the men didn't speak either; the fatigue of the journey had exhausted what little desire to speak they had shown at the outset. They went for whole days without talking, without the exchange of a single syllable among those hundreds of soldiers and convicts.

"Everything is thought," said Duval to himself. "Language doesn't exist."

He let that inhuman serenity enter him and then expelled it with an idea: "Everything is possible. If language doesn't exist, everything is possible. I'm allowed to do anything."

In those long hours of rain and calm, the distant screeching of a bird hidden in the scrub or high in the sky, the sharp cry of a lapwing or a buzzard, served only to accentuate the silent stillness of the landscape.

Nothing on the horizon, day after day. The soldiers rode on and discharged their duties with supreme indifference. Duval had long given up trying to make friends with them. To him they seemed alien, and they were, necessarily, as he was now coming to understand. The soldiers were ex-convicts (like the ones chained in the wagons), who had survived by forfeiting God knows what to the rigors of frontier life, and had managed to adapt to the futility of army routine. Only the pursuit of game stirred them into activity: chasing a rhea with their bolas, or skinning a tremulous Patagonian hare. Sometimes they deigned to consort with the female prisoners, when Lieutenant Lavalle felt like granting his men the dubious pleasure of choosing a partner for the night and had the women unchained so that they could be taken off and enjoyed under cover of darkness.

The silence was manifest in everything; it appeared and disappeared, soft as the air and sometimes hard as stone. Duval breathed, deeply; he breathed as he had never done before, with a kind of tentative belief in life's reality. At this point in the boredom of the journey, the engineer was suddenly surprised to find himself counting his breaths. He felt that he had discovered the most primitive use of numbers, and thought that if he could keep count of those movements of subtle air, he would arrive at the number of the earth, and silence, and the horses' fear, and he went on murmuring nebulous numbers to the rhythms of his chest and head. In fact he had lost count right from the start, but that didn't stop him feeling that it was, precisely, a calculation. He liked to think of it not as an accumulation over time but as the determination of a fundamental unit: a precise, slow, motionless division that he was performing with atmospheric silences. The mathematical fantasies that made the trivial tedium of life in the desert bearable found their natural object in breath's little butterflies, in that double constancy: inhalation, exhalation.

As he rode into the setting sun, Duval counted, with his watch in his hand. He was trying to work out, approximately of course, how many breaths he had taken since he was born. He imagined the almost insect-like system of specific muscles activated over and over to draw in and then expel the air. It would not be hard to build a machine that would work like that indefinitely, but what use would it be? Set up, for example, on one of those vast plains they were crossing, it would be forgotten for a thousand years ... Though a more artistic solution, he thought, would be to leave something to *represent* the machine: a stone, for example (anything would do); he imagined it oblong in shape, the size of a large rat ... For a moment he could almost see it, vividly there. Caught up in these daydreams, he forgot that he was breathing, and then remembered, with a smile.

None of his fantasies, however, prepared him for the event that would take place a few days later: a manifestation of silence, rather disturbing perhaps, but at least it broke the monotony and gave him something new to think about.

One afternoon they spied something far off to the south: a strip of land that seemed to be billowing. No dust rose for the simple reason that, after the saturating rains, there was none on the ground. Everyone seemed to know what it was, except for Duval, who spurred his horse and caught up with the lieutenant.

"The she-dogs!" said the soldiers.

"Les chiennes?" he asked Lavalle, amazed.

A look of irritation twisted the Lieutenant's mouth.

"Another absurd contingency, as if there weren't enough," he replied grumpily. He seemed to be exasperated by this new development, but there was a weariness to his disgust. It was as if he thought of the plains as a theatre for idiotic events, and this was the straw that had broken the back of his patience.

It was a pack of wild she-dogs, familiarly known as sea lions, and not at all dangerous, Lavalle condescended to reveal, as long as certain basic precautions were taken.

Duval looked at the horizon again. There must have been a

great many of them. But no one seemed to be alarmed, except for the horses, quick to sense the emanations of those creatures and trembling more than usual. The soldiers, it seemed, would not bother to hunt them (perhaps they were not edible). The pack kept drawing closer, and given the direction in which it was moving, Duval reckoned it would come very close. It was absurd, but he didn't care. Those sea lions were not afraid of human beings.

The dogs approached without a sound; they too must have been mute. Although, listening carefully, one could hear a raspy buzzing, made perhaps by their paws on the ground.

Within half an hour Duval could see the sea lions clearly: they were large, slim dogs, similar to greyhounds, all gray in color, with pointed muzzles, long, catlike tails that dragged piti-fully, and no ears, hence the name. Their gait was awkward; they lumbered along with a heaviness paradoxical in such dainty creatures. Their clumsiness seemed an affectation, al-most a surplus of elegance. But how could they hear? Up until then Duval had believed that all mammals had ears.

Finally the dogs came within a few yards of the humans and horses, passing without so much as a glance. Such a degree of indifference could not be achieved from one day to the next. Seen at close range, their eyes were the most striking thing about them: they were lidless; the pupil floated in a pink oval, without an iris; and the heavy bags hanging underneath gave them a sinister air. They were like the eyes of an old alcoholic, except that they were on opposite sides of the head and both could not be seen at once. The travelers were overwhelmed by the dogs' smell: a sort of faint civet, yet it filled heaven and earth. Duval's horse was writhing hysterically, threatening to topple him; he pressed his palms against its neck, trying to calm it down. The soldiers were less considerate; they stunned their mounts with vigorous punching. Duval slowed down and fell back gradually until he was level with one of the last wagons. The prisoners were looking at the sea lions with disdain. Suddenly Duval heard the crying of a child; he turned his gaze from the spectacle of the pack and searched for the source of that very faint sound among the wagon's equally spectral passengers. Almost all the babies that had come with the women had died in the course of the journey. By the time Duval spied this one, his mother had hushed him by putting a nipple into his mouth; the baby sucked automatically for a moment, then fell asleep. The woman looked up into the Frenchman's eyes ...

Duval was disconcerted. He didn't know if it was because of the unearthly silence or the deep strangeness of the situation or because of some special quality in those distant, catatonic eyes. The woman was wearing the tattered remains of two different dresses and she was so small, so thin and wasted, that she could have been taken for a child. Under a thick layer of filth, her features looked African, and her hair was short, bristling and greasy.

As they left the dogs behind, a melancholy feeling came over the Frenchman. Everything was so futile. This state of mind must have been obvious to the lieutenant, who offered him a swig of brandy.

"Where could they have come from?" asked Duval.

Lavalle shrugged his shoulders.

"You don't hunt them?"

"Occasionally, very occasionally, the men organize a hunting party. I've been told that the dogs' rumps make very good steaks, but I've never tried them. If we were short of food, a pack like that could feed the troop for months. Apparently the fat is useful too."

"I don't think they'd have much. You can see their skeletons."

"True. They're always on the move, even when they're asleep; that's why they need a reserve of fat, and because there's so little it's especially rich. They live on insects, toads, snakes ..."

"I'd like to have one."

"They are quite decorative, it's true. I know this is hard to believe, but they belong to the same family as seals. Did you notice that they don't have ears? But I don't think they could be tamed, they're so indifferent ..."

They went on talking for some time; the lieutenant was in an unusually sociable mood. The drizzle had resumed after about thirty hours of respite. Against a dark background of clouds, the air shone, full of crystalline droplets. Lavalle handed Duval his cigar case, which the Frenchman examined; he was astonished to see such pure silver, without the slightest trace of gray.

"It's white gold," said the lieutenant, putting it back into his trouser pocket. He launched into a rambling story about the woman who had given it to him, but stopped when he noticed that the Frenchman was miles away, ignoring his lewd tale. Duval was thinking about the convict woman.

"Isn't there some other way to bring women out here? Wouldn't some be prepared to follow their husbands?"

"No."

"Maybe they would."

"It makes no difference, anyway. Willingly or against their will, they have a function to perform: satisfying the men. Men, on the other hand, have no function in nature. Take us, for example. What are we doing here? Who could say? But the women … They change."

"Change? Into what?"

"Who knows? And anyway, that doesn't matter either. They are muses. There are many possibilities … For some reason best known to themselves, the Indians prize white women as tokens of exchange, so once they cross the frontier, they begin to 'circulate' in all kinds of deals …"

"Do you mean," exclaimed the Frenchman, "that they're *sold* to the savages?"

"There's no need to be shocked. Some are taken captive, or a soldier might exchange his wife for horses, or a commander might even present a chief with a bevy of beauties as a token of good will. And that introduces them into a world where they become a form of currency."

"It seems dreadfully callous."

"You'll change your mind, I assure you. These women, as I

suppose you will have noticed already, are entirely at our disposal; that's why I used the word 'muses.' Life or death, a white husband or an Indian: for them it's all the same. You must remember that society has cast them out in the harshest possible manner, leaving them without a destiny, as it were; and the way the Indians use them has precisely the effect of prolonging that suspension, perhaps for the rest of their lives. Poetic, isn't it?"

This attempt at speculation exasperated Duval.

"Could there really be crimes so serious as to merit such a punishment?"

"They've committed trifling misdemeanors, not serious crimes. The punishment is inversely proportional."

"I don't understand."

With a grave air, Lavalle inhaled the smoke of his cigar. He declined to explain.

"It's a commonplace in ethnology: the much-discussed exchange of women. When you see it for yourself, you'll realize how harmless it is: an innocent spectacle, and rather pointless, really, like everything else."

The Frenchman's mind was wandering again.

"I noticed one of them today ... She wasn't the kind of woman who could save a man. Some are too innocuous."

The lieutenant began to laugh but checked himself and threw a sidelong glance at Duval.

"I hadn't imagined that you might be interested in one of our passengers. Would you like her?" he asked with his characteristic bluntness. "Which wagon is she in?"

"No, no!" the Frenchman hastened to exclaim. "She looked like a frail old woman …"

He said no more—the lieutenant was smoking ironically—and regretted having voiced his thoughts.

That night, as he went for his usual walk around the convoy to stretch his legs, Duval saw the prisoners being unloaded so that they could spend the night on the ground and take a few steps: their daily exercise. They would have preferred to sleep where they had spent that day and all the previous days, and were offering passive resistance, so they had to be forcibly dislodged. It was not yet completely dark; the luxurious gray of the rain was shining in the twilight. The soldiers climbed up the rails of the wagons like monkeys, unfastened the fettering chains and tossed the ends down to their companions, who brutally dragged the prisoners out. Like a sleepwalker, Duval went along counting the wagons, seeing the same scene repeated, until he reached one near the end of the train.

Still visible in that half-light, the convicts were grotesque figures: almost naked, with stick-thin limbs and swollen bellies, moving awkwardly, against their will. The women looked like emaciated dwarves or dolls. After a while, only their silhouettes could be seen, and the occasional glistening of wet chains. No one shouted. The silence was leavened by interjections and moans.

Straight away Duval recognized the woman he had seen before, though she was no more than a fragile outline … But he felt that he was being observed in turn by Lavalle's equestrian shadow. He glimpsed the lieutenant's smile, pearly with liquor; it was clear from the way his murmuring eyes were fixed on the black-on-black commotion of the convicts that he had followed the Frenchman's gaze and spied the woman simultaneously, or first, perhaps. Duval moved away immediately and stopped to observe the unloading of the next wagon in a futile attempt to feign indifference. Lavalle had gone in the opposite direction.

During the afternoon, the soldiers had hunted partridges and quail-doves, which they had piled up on ponchos. They were plucking them hastily by the light of the fires, and skewering them on spits for roasting. To everyone's surprise the lieutenant shared out a barrel of brandy. He uncorked a bottle of champagne that he had chilled with wet paper and balsam leaves, and with sarcastic courtesy invited the Frenchman to share it.

The birds, it turned out, were delicious. After several days of living on biscuits and the occasional strip of jerky, it was heartening for Duval to eat those tender white breasts and wings. Lavalle encouraged him to drink glass after glass of champagne, and became disturbingly voluble.

Duval suspected that he was planning some kind of mischief. And he was not mistaken. As soon as the lieutenant finished his dinner—the men were lapsing into drunken torpor, hunched around the fires—he announced to his aide that he would graciously permit his soldiers to take the convict women of their choice and have their way with them. The news spread. Fired up by the brandy and the prospect of a night's abuse, the men stumbled over to the wagons, breathing heavily.

There was a moment of confusion, during which Lavalle disappeared, and Duval took the opportunity to move his bedroll as far away as possible and lie down, regretting that for reasons of safety he could not sleep outside the circle of sentries, beyond sight and earshot of that scandal. He had not been lying down for a minute when he saw a woman approaching him. Barefoot, she moved like a tiny, dark, deranged cloud. The light of a fire revealed her features and her half-closed eyes. Even before that, he had recognized her. She became a shadow again. Then she kneeled down a few yards away. Duval knew that she had been sent by the succubus, that she was another of his tricks. He remained as still as a piece of furniture. The woman laid the sleeping baby that she had been carrying on the ground, then came and lay down beside him. The Frenchman looked around vaguely. He must have fallen asleep for a while without noticing, because the camp was very quiet. On the closest bedrolls the officers were groaning and writhing on top of the women, pounding and rocking, but everything had swiveled imperceptibly in the silence, and to Duval it all seemed remote. She was indeed the smallest woman he had ever seen; it had not been an illusory effect of distance. She was in his arms. They coupled. After the act, the engineer took the precaution of washing himself vigorously with brandy from his hipflask.

Two or three hours later he was woken by the light of the rising moon. The night became a sort of day, sad and deserted like the days themselves. Everyone was sleeping; there was not a sound. He turned cautiously toward the woman, and saw that she was very young, perhaps just a girl. He did not touch her, but it was as if she had felt his gaze; her eyes opened and looked into his without any expression, mute and clear. Then she turned to look at the child, who was sleeping peacefully. The Frenchman was carried off by an irresistible drowsiness.

At dawn, she was gone. During the day he kept away from the rear wagons. He would also have liked to avoid Lavalle, but the lieutenant seemed to seek out his company with the sole intent of laughing sadistically into his ear.

The woman returned to him that night, and the next, even though permission to take the female prisoners aside had not been renewed. She and Duval did not speak. He did not even discover her name. She was revealed to him by the moonlight: impassive, with asymmetrical African or Indian features that made her seem permanently distracted or remote. There was something childlike in her gaze; she always seemed to be thinking about something else. Her lips were full and protuberant. Sometimes he woke before dawn and saw her breast-feeding the child. Her small breasts seemed to contain an inexhaustible supply. The Frenchman was entering a world of anxiety, fear and brooding. But the girl disappeared from his mind with the same light steps that brought her into the world.

On the fourth or fifth night the lieutenant had her brought to his own bedroll, before the others had turned in. He took her straight away, in sight of the officers, who went on drinking without saying a word. The engineer was stunned; for a moment, shock held him like a web from which he had to struggle free before he could get up and drag his sleeping bag as far away as possible. Even so, her cries kept him awake. The following morning, Lavalle rode up to the Frenchman's horse and offered him a cigarette. Duval thought that he was going to excuse himself for what had happened the night before, but no. Lavalle didn't seem to remember anything.

The rains had finally stopped. The atmosphere of quiet neutrality gave way to a more conventional animation: birds flying about in the sky, trilling in all manner of ways; enormous flocks of cheeping partridges; the dry breathy noise of rheas' wings ... And nights full of the whistling of foxes and the chattering of crickets. The soldiers suddenly became talkative, telling stories and cracking jokes incessantly around the campfires or on horseback, spouting puerile lies with the naivety of the truly barbaric. The nights were warm, and now they had permission from the lieutenant to satisfy their desires with the women whenever they liked. The officers' favorite was a voluptuous prostitute who wore her hair piled up like an ovenbird's nest and had been on edge ever since her new situation had forced her to give up smoking.

But the journey was already approaching its end. Scouting ahead, an advance party sighted a river, which meant that they were near Pringles: from there it would be only ten days. To reach that river, they marched for a whole day without resting. As they drew near, they could hear the clamor of the birds; there were tall willows by the water's edge, swaying in the breeze. Lavalle announced his decision to stay there the next day as well, since the troop and the animals would need a rest before embarking on the final leg.

Duval wandered off as soon as they arrived; what he required to help him recover was a little solitude. He was heartily sick of people. There were too many gazes on the pampa and not enough confined spaces. He followed the bank of the river. The sharp-edged willow leaves hung in walls, providing a glorious shelter. The water flowed deep and slow in the shade. It was a personal labyrinth; he was just coming to realize how tense he had been. A dip, he thought, would do him good, although by that stage in the afternoon, it was no longer hot.

When he plunged in, he was taken aback by the coldness of the water, and for a moment he couldn't breathe. But he swam vigorously to get his blood moving again, and then it was pleasant. Climbing out, he sank into the mud, and had to hold onto the three-sided reeds. After the water, the breeze felt mild; it enveloped him in comforting caresses. He sat on a rock and washed the mud off his legs, then lay down on the grass, in a place where the yellow sunlight was falling. He tried to identify the birds by their songs, unsuccessfully. He had been told that each kind of bird sang the song of another kind, never that of its own.

He could hear the soldiers shouting in the distance. They must have been swimming too, or washing the horses.

A white and pink echidna came crawling up the bank but went back into the water when it saw him.

Duval lit his pipe and smoked for a while, until the sun went completely red. Then he got dressed, unhurriedly, and began to walk back. He heard a tremendous uproar coming from the camp, so loud that he wondered for a moment if they hadn't been ambushed. But then he heard laughter and the joyful shrieking of women's voices. He suspected some prank on the part of the gauchos. Impelled by curiosity, he hurried on and, emerging from the undergrowth, was greatly surprised to find the soldiers in the river, forcibly bathing the women. The water at the fording place came up to their knees. In one big joyful frenzy, the men were using large bars of soap to cover the women with lather, then dunking them. If any tried to escape to the bank, they were pulled back in. The game had aroused the men, and the girls were rosy from giggling, full of wild charm.

Lieutenant Lavalle, his clothes in a mess, was on the bank, reclining on a pink rock the size and shape of a crocodile, smoking and roaring with laughter. With a leer he cried out, telling the soldiers to take the women off into the bushes, since they would be on guard duty that night. There was a moment of silence. The sun had reddened both the water and the bodies emerging from it, casting a splendor already tempered by intimations of the suave and compact darkness to come. It was a moment of silence and tense, expectant stillness but there was no need to repeat the invitation: without drying off, the bathers disappeared into the tall grass on both banks of the river, and after a while began to reemerge, smiling stupidly, unsteady on their legs.

They still had time to hunt a few small animals—beavers,

otters, ducks—and the most adroit among them pursued black eels that were said to be very tasty. With the last light, they set up the spits and lit the fires. Lavalle, who had been drinking all afternoon and was more gone than usual, insisted that they build a bonfire on top of his mauve rock, and invited Duval to sit and dine with him. They rested their backs against the slightly coiled tail of that crocodile-like form, and the water's bluish aura, or perhaps their sense of wellbeing, led them to adopt almost feminine poses. The aides pulled up a net containing bottles that had been left to chill in an icy pool. Then they brought the roasted game, which the lieutenant did not touch. The conversation was rather incoherent, and his gaze, adorned with tiny inverted flames, was sinister.

It was an early, hurried dinner. As soon as the first really dense shadows gathered, the night watch began, with five times as many sentries as usual because the situation was especially perilous: they were surrounded by screens of quiet trees, but in that quiet was a whispering which could also hide things. It was the ideal place for an ambush, if you thought about it: the Indians would emerge from the camouflage with phosphorescent cheekbones and teeth painted black. The soldiers slipped away under the stars to take up their positions. Suddenly, the terrible din of the frogs began. A toad would occasionally interrupt them with mournful laughter, but then the little frogs resumed their song. Lavalle's mood took a grotesque turn: he started laughing and cracking jokes, smoked a cigarette to put himself to sleep, then began to yell, giving the order to bring "the engineer's fiancée." Two soldiers, who were getting drunk beneath the stone reptile ran off to find her, and drag her no doubt from the arms of some corporal.

It was, after all, a good excuse to escape from that drunkard's insolent company. Duval took the woman as far away as he could, without going beyond the ring of sentries.

The night was perfect. All the unknown constellations shone and glided through the gigantic sky, and when the moon came out, it covered the world with its dark pallor, which rouses some people and sends the rest to sleep. The frogs fell silent; then the moths and crickets sang, and when they too fell silent there was only the whistling of the owls in the overall quiet. Sleep and waking.

Duval woke up with the first light of dawn, when the moon had already gone down. The girl was breast-feeding her child. Not a bird was singing. The stars, in their frozen swirls, had not even begun to grow faint. Her eyes were half closed and her arms were pink. The Frenchman watched her intently. The child's hand was moving on his mother's breast; eventually he fell asleep. She laid him on a folded blanket and stretched out on the bedroll again. She didn't look up. But their eyes met for a moment. Faced with her impassive gaze, he felt cumbersomely expressive, almost like the horses.

Reveille had been delayed for an hour, so they could go on sleeping or thinking. Feminine impassiveness, Duval reflected, is an effect of submission; a man, by contrast, is expressive because he never puts himself at another man's disposal. What about the Indians? Perhaps he would have something to learn from them in that regard ...

The travelers had a day of rest, which they spent on the knolls by the river or in the water. They washed their clothes and the horses. At midday the grass was covered with white shirts drying, and the pink and gray coats of the horses shone, clean and bristling.

Breakfast was so plentiful and long it almost flowed into lunch. The soldiers amused themselves fishing and searching for nests. The river water chilled the drinks. The men took a siesta with the women, slept soundly, and as they gradually woke up in the mid-afternoon, the lieutenant ordered them to set off, since he didn't want to spend another night in such a dangerous place. He rode beside Duval, who questioned him about their destination with boyish curiosity. Lavalle was less cynical than usual. What was it like, the famed Pillahuinco, the river there in Pringles? Was it like the one they were leaving behind? The Frenchman had found it bucolic.

The Argentine whistled briefly.

"A paradise. This little valley is nothing, a moment. The other one is as big as a whole lifetime: a gigantic, everlasting Eden. But dangerous: the forest stretches for thousands of leagues, no one knows quite how far, and it's teeming with savages, all sorts of wandering tribes, skilled in the use of deadly poisons. It's only by a miracle that the fort has held out, on the very edge of the forest, so you can imagine what it would be like for a man on his own in there."

A thoughtful silence ensued. The Frenchman was wondering: "What's the danger?"

The next morning the woods were out of sight behind them and they were advancing across an empty prairie again. They were counting the days and the hours in fervent anticipation. Even the convicts seemed to perk up. The last days were sunny; it was almost summer. When the air was clear they could see flocks of birds in the distance descending toward the forest. The great torpor of the journey was disintegrating like a color seen from very close up. The Frenchman was thinking of the danger ahead, and of the frontier, which he imagined as a limitless territory, where his route would allow for any interruption, granting him at every step a new and joyful entry—but he would have to learn how to move all over again, like a dancer, submitting to a strict discipline, so as not to stop for a single moment in that mysterious web. Sometimes, in the tides of thought that he allowed to rise within him, the forest appeared as a veil, imperfectly concealing other scenes, and the images of politics. Immoral politics scattered the landscape with living statues. He was intoxicated by the peculiar combination of nature and Machiavellianism.

On the penultimate day, dense flocks of flamingos flew overhead with an oppressive baroque neutrality, and clouds of small gray birds rose from the ground, obscuring the way ahead. The convicts scanned the horizon curiously. Lavalle was drinking and in a bad mood. Duval was in his private space.

His work as an engineer was like springtime's transformation of the world. He shuddered with nameless, urgent needs, and a growing restlessness set his spine tingling. What was he supposed to do there at the edge of the world? For the moment, only Espina knew. But he cherished the hope that the task assigned to him would be all-encompassing and absorb his life entirely. He could not, in that state of mind, have found satisfaction in anything less sublime.

SHE WAS WOKEN BY THE SILENCE THAT FOLLOWED A trill from the tremulous beak of a nearby bird. It must have been late, to judge from the vertical strips of brightness at the edges of the paper curtains. But the child was fast asleep in the basket. Ema closed her eyes and turned over under the sheet without waking her husband. She gripped the edge of the blanket and gave it a quick shake: it puffed up into a soft dome, which then collapsed in slow motion, tepidly wedding their forms. Her husband was sleeping with his mouth open, breathing heavily, and Ema could feel his radiant warmth. She fell asleep but was woken again by the child crying, and this time she went to look at him: he was wriggling in the basket with his eyes still closed. She calmed him by stroking his forehead and murmuring a few words. Then she lifted her head and looked around.

She slid aside the osier stick from which two sheets of paper—serving as a door—were hung, and went out onto the veranda of the hut. It was earlier than she had supposed: there was still an hour to go before the sun would rise and dispel the lingering cool, which seeped through the light fabric of her nightgown and made her shiver. She felt the baby stirring in her womb. It generally woke at that hour. She would give birth in four months' time, at the end of the winter that had not yet begun.

Between two erratic rows of huts, the street was empty. No one was up, not even the animals. A few windmills, with stationary sails. The faraway moon, almost transparent, the size of a head, already very low. Some thin clouds were drifting across the sky; she saw them suddenly turn pink, and just then the trilling that had woken her began again, glassy and prolonged: a goldfinch. With a ball of fat suspended from the eaves, she had attracted a white-banded mockingbird which sang for the family, sometimes all day long, but it was shy. Unlike the goldfinches, with their green and gray wings, which had befriended her and would come to eat seeds from her hand. Which of them was singing? She couldn't see.

She thought of going to get something for breakfast. Her husband would not wake up until it was time for him to return to the barracks; yesterday had been his day off duty, and he had spent it drinking and playing dice.

As quietly as she had stepped out, she went back in and put on a dress that had been made by the Indian women, like all the clothing in the village. She put the basket on the table and contemplated the child, Francisco, who was sighing: finally he opened his eyes, looking very serious. Perhaps he wasn't happy to have woken up. But when Ema picked him up and murmured something, he laughed sleepily. He was already ten months old. Slim and small, he appeared more fragile than he really was. His dark hair was very long and fine. Ema picked him up, unfolded the screens, placing them in front of the windows so that the light would not wake Gombo, and went out. Francisco rubbed his eyes violently.

She set off walking unhurriedly along the empty street. Noises could be heard from the huts: a word, a baby crying for the breast. One of the many hares that the children of the village kept as pets came running toward Ema, stopped, and sat down to look at her. In a while, when the sun came up, they would turn and gaze at it intently, becoming easy prey for the horses, which ate them.

A disheveled woman emerged from a hut, wearing a white dress she seemed to have slept in, it was so thoroughly crushed. She stopped on the threshold, bewildered and dazzled. Ema's greeting startled her. When she saw who it was, she asked Ema to wait, ran inside, and came straight out again, holding a sleeping baby and a brush, with which she absently tidied her mop of hair. They set off together for the river, as the village around them was beginning to show the first signs of life. Reveille had not yet sounded from the fort but it would not be long. The soldiers were leaving the huts to report for duty, just in time, moving like sleepwalkers, burdened by their hangovers. They saw nothing, not even the day. It would take them a good part of the morning to recover. Some women, however, were returning from the fields by the river with buckets of milk.

A sleepy soldier had come out onto the veranda of his house and stopped there, right on the edge, to pee, swaying dangerously.

As the two women came over one of the hills on which the village had been built, the fort appeared before them, a sprawling edifice, with a breadth of roughly two hundred yards, its high bamboo palisades surmounted by towers at each of the four corners and the lookout, where a sentry was drowsing.

The women turned their gaze toward the horizon beyond the river: the sky's invisible spirals stretched away into the deep distance. Remote updrafts carried columns of birds up and up until they plunged from the top of that antigravitational fall, their far cries, some as small as pips, leaping about with a life of their own.

The fields, as they did every morning, presented a colorful, variegated scene. To the right, along the edge of the forest, was the camp of the "tame" Indians under the protection of the fort. By that hour, they had been up and about for a long time. They were gathering to milk their little white cows and lighting fires, beside which, after bathing, they would spend the whole morning having breakfast and smoking. At dawn the water was warmer than the air, and from the moment the first light appeared in the east, they all went swimming for the pleasure of it. The grass was still shining with dew, and there they would lie down afterward and dry themselves in the waves of radiant heat from the fires, which the smoke from their cigarettes made visible. As Ema and her friend approached, a group of about thirty savages emerged from the river, shaking themselves and shouting joyfully. Beside a big fire on which water was being boiled for coffee and tea, they lit up their first cigarettes and took deep, voluptuous breaths of smoke.

The women went their separate ways, Ema's friend heading for a circle of Indians, while Ema went to the river to wash her baby. She sat on a rock with her feet in the water, beyond the place where the children played. The tepid, roundabout flow wet her skin. She cupped a few drops in her hand and washed Francisco's face. He wriggled. It was quiet and calm; she let a daydream carry her away. Suddenly, right in front of them, almost between Ema's feet, the head of an Indian emerged from the water; he had approached below the surface to surprise her. A face with asymmetrical features, a huge mouth, and the squinting eyes that were so common among the savages. The head ducked under again, then reappeared, with consummate agility, laughing all the while. A clown. Or could it have been a severed head, propelled by the diabolical force of laughter? But suddenly the Indian stretched out and floated, and the whole of his powerful body shone for a few seconds, surrounded by a nimbus of spreading ripples. Then he swam away.

In the middle of the middle of the pool, the Indians were fishing with creels and sharpened sticks. Before dawn, the children went out searching for the coveted freshwater molluscs, which the birds could find only in full daylight, hours later. The banks must have been stripped clean that day, because the heron-ibis and the kingfishers could be heard complaining hoarsely from the trees. Perhaps they were hungry, and waiting for an opportunity to steal something.

Ema looked around. The girls carried tiny combs, hanging from necklaces, against their napes, so that they could always ensure that their black hair was perfectly straight. She borrowed one from a girl who was passing and carefully combed Francisco's hair. After which she went to one of the circles where breakfast was being cooked. Various Indians of both sexes, as well as two or three white women, were waiting as big fish, splayed and symmetrical like butterflies, roasted on spits. They offered her wild melons the size of apples and sour to the taste.

She took a tiny egg from a raffia box, intrigued.

"Are they partridge eggs?" she asked the Indian woman beside her.

"No. Guinea fowl. Take as many as you like."

American guinea fowl are smaller than the African variety, almost like seagulls, and their thimble-size eggs are gray-green with a red spot on top. Ema broke two into a cup of milk that had been handed to her, stirred them in until the liquid took on a yellowish color, and Francisco drank it conscientiously, down to the last drop. The Indian men were returning from the river with wet hair. Ema drank a cup of milk herself and rolled a cigarette, her first for the day. She inhaled deeply with her eyes closed, and waited before sending up a long shaft of smoke. The sun had already risen. It was shining on the plain across the river. Finally, all the birds began to sing, forgetting their wretchedness. Daytime happiness possessed them irresistibly. Even the conversations of the crows seemed cheerful. The fish were ready. They were sprinkled with salt and white vinegar. Ema ate half of one and drank a little cup of berry liqueur. The women rolled cigarettes and, with a characteristic movement, held them for the men to draw on. More people kept arriving, including soldiers who went swimming, or drank and smoked beside the fires. They had big bags under their eyes and were deathly pale: they must have been up all night gambling, and now they were coming for a snack before going to sleep or resuming duty.

Suddenly two horsemen appeared, attracting everyone's attention: two Indians, deputy chiefs, no doubt, riding small gray mares, chosen for the way their pale color contrasted with the riders, who were painted from head to foot. Without dismounting, they approached some bathers, with whom they conversed for a moment and laughed hoarsely. Everyone was pretending to ignore them.

"Who are they?" Ema asked the Indian man sitting beside her, who, in a show of good manners, had not so much as glanced in their direction.

"Two of Caful's nephews; I don't know what they're called, but I bet their parents, who are always sucking up to the chief, have given them ridiculous names like Baúl or Raúl, or something like that," he said, and burst out laughing.

"Did they come from the fort?"

"They must have been gambling all night, and now they're going back to their uncle's camp to sleep."

Caful's settlement lay some leagues away. The accord between the neighboring groups was strange and complex, and the cunning chief contrived to complicate it further day by day. Who could tell what crafty diplomatic gambit had determined the visit of the two princes? They were truly splendid, thought Ema: small and handsome, with their bodies vanishing under the paint and their long, black, oiled hair. Modern rifles hung from their saddles.

A good while later, she set off back to the village, alone. She had left the baby with some Indian girls, who liked to play at captives all day long. She was carrying her provisions in a bag: eggs, mushrooms, milk, and a tin of tea.

The hut was as she had left it, with the curtains drawn close and the screens extended. She went in quietly. Gombo was sleeping; she did not wake him. But his sleep was lighter now, nearing its end, so she set about getting something ready for his late breakfast. She made flatbread with mushrooms and chili, splayed the fish and doused them with brandy to prepare them for frying. When it was all ready she went and sat down beside the sleeping man's head. He was stirring and about to wake. Gombo was a gaucho, about thirty-five years old, with very deep wrinkles for his age, long hair, and a full pepper-and-salt beard. He was dreaming of something.

Taking her time, Ema prepared a large cigar, with a leaf that she rolled and unrolled several times, and a mixture of herbs that she took from a small box. Holding it between her lips, she lit it and puffed a couple of times, surrounding herself and the sleeping man with a little cloud. The smell finally woke him; he opened his eyes and looked at her blankly. Ema took his head in one hand and lifted it slightly, then rested it on her thigh. She put the cigar in his mouth, and took it out a moment later, without waiting for him to inhale, repeating this operation over and over, until he gradually came back to life, adjusting the rhythm of his breathing to the smouldering of that thick roll of herbs.

Eventually the clouds of dense, pungent smoke, as big as atmospheric clouds, found their way into his lungs and infiltrated the blood heading for his brain.

The state of his eyes spoke eloquently of the previous night's intemperance.

"Are you awake?" she asked.

He uttered an incomprehensible word and coughed. She raised a cup of milk to his lips and held it there while he drank. He had no appetite, and would probably not eat anything during his days on duty at the barracks. The soldiers ran on cigarettes and alcohol, in general. Propped against his wife's belly, Gombo was startled by a sudden watery movement.

"What time is it?" he asked.

"There's time," she replied, and went to put the fish on the fire.

He asked after the baby. Sitting on the rush mat in his underpants, he brushed his hair and beard, stretching incessantly. Ema asked about Caful's two nephews, who had intrigued her.

"Where did you see them?"

"By the river, just then. They came from the fort on two little gray mares, and people said they were going back to their uncle's camp."

Gombo sighed: "They come to gamble, loaded with gold and agate. They must have lost everything, otherwise they would have bought horses."

For a moment he remained pensive.

"Although they might have other reasons. They say Caful is negotiating a new peace agreement with Espina. There have been a lot of visits in the last few weeks."

"But isn't there peace already?"

"I guess Espina wants a more complicated, more delicate kind of peace."

He got up and opened the windows. The sky was white and overcast, and the increasing sultriness of the air indicated that a storm was on the way. He went out onto the veranda and whistled at the birds. There he unfolded a table and two chairs.

Ema brought a basket of bread, the fish, scrambled eggs, a bottle of white wine, and a bowl of washed fruit. They ate at leisure, chatting.

When he had gone, she went back inside and washed up in a few minutes, folded the rush mats on which they slept, and put them away in a chest.

Then, with nothing to do — it was too hot inside for a siesta — she went out into the hut's tiny sunken garden, where she had planted some cuttings and bulbs. The anemones were the last flowers of summer, but they were not yet open. She regretted not having watered them earlier. If she did it now the sun would burn them. But the earth was parched, and the dead shells of bugs bore witness to the drought.

A yellowy-gray cat with a black face came slinking up. He looked at her and meowed. Finding him one day in the forest, she had been surprised to see such a delicate animal roaming free and starved half to death; he must have been the pet of some Indian concubine. The birds hated him, not without reason; he was a hunter, but didn't eat his victims, living instead on the pieces of cooked meat that Ema sometimes remembered to give him.

Hours later, she went to the river to fetch Francisco. She found the girls under a neem tree; they had given the baby milk and berries, and offered to look after him until nightfall. Ema walked away along the bank, her prominent belly swaying, in search of a cool place where she could wait for sunset. The arm of the river bent around, and there was a little stone bridge, in the shade of which echidnas were playing. She watched them for a moment, charmed by the uncoordinated movements of those spiny little creatures. When she made up her mind to go on, she took a path that led into a dense grove. The trees were quiet; the birds must have been napping. The air was conducive to sleep.

A little further on she came to a beach, where she found ten young people swimming and sleeping. Since she often went wandering along the edges of the forest, they knew her. She sat down on the grass, next to an Indian girl who was also pregnant, and they chatted for a while. At that spot, just a few threads of sunlight filtered by the greenery penetrated the shade. Ema lay back and almost closed her eyes; through the little slits left open she could see points of green light moving high above, a luminous, golden green, with mossy shadows and sometimes a gentle, fantastic explosion of the summer sky's polished blue, or a streak of colorless light.

In the distance she could hear the voices of the youths, who were playing dice. Delicate little ducks were splashing about on the surface of the river. The rustling in the domes of foliage lulled her to sleep.

When she woke up, the light was fading. Some of the Indians had gone back into the water, others were drowsing on the grass, and they were all smoking. Ema smoked a cigarette too and then took her leave. She made her way back as slowly as possible. When she came down from the hill, she saw the vast colors of the sky over the plains. The rusty red hue of the clouds that were rising in the east could not disguise their threatening burden: it would rain that night. Among the pinks and violets, she saw Venus appear in the west, shining brightly, surrounded by gray haloes. It was already night as she walked down the village's single street toward her hut.

The girls were waiting for her on the veranda holding Francisco, who was sound asleep. She was pleased to see them. It would have been annoying to have to search them out, weary as she was. She invited them in to drink what was left of the milk. They helped her to draw the curtains, and lit the lamp without being asked. She said they could stay the night, since she was on her own. Then they showed her what they had brought in a bag: fat, transparent river snails in their twisted shells. They put them on to boil with herbs, and very soon the hut was full of a delicious smell. They sat down around the table with big white china plates in front them, thick and heavy as stone.

After dining and putting the baby to bed, Ema and the girls

went out onto the veranda to get some fresh air before turning in. The moon was rising, veiled by peculiar storm clouds. A threatening wind began to blow, and they felt flurries of birds passing over the huts. Lightning flashed, and a moment later the first drops of rain fell with the force of bullets, making the girls rush inside. But Ema stayed a moment longer on her own.

She was thinking of the night of the Monkey Festival, the first time she had left the fort, and the fear she had felt on that occasion, faced with the limitless chaos of life. But even then, and perhaps for a long time before that, Ema had known that her life was destined to unfold in the midst of strangeness simply because of the century into which she had been born. Barely out of childhood and alone in the world with her baby, she found herself banished to a dangerous and ill-defined frontier. The epoch demanded absolute calm; humans had to become as impassive as animals.

The flashes of lightning entertained her; they were so unpredictable. All that she remembered vanished in an instant. The light revealed nothing but its own futility.

On arriving in Pringles after the exhausting journey through the desert, Ema and another very young convict woman had been taken aside and handed over to two officers. The one she ended up with was a lieutenant whose surname was Paz: a carefree young man, perpetually drunk, with the health of a hardy animal and imperturbable in sleep. When he received Ema, he dismissed the wife he already had. His lodgings, like those of all the other officers, were above the casino. The doors opened onto a corridor that led to the main salon. Paz had the use of two large, carpeted rooms, full of old, dark objects, including a mahogany tub in which he took two long baths each day.

For Ema, it was a life of confinement, since she only left the apartment to gather with the other women in the corridors or neighboring rooms. They never went down into the street. From the windows she could see only the inside of the palisade and the sky above. In any case, they lived by night and slept all day with the curtains drawn. She found that life poetic and pleasurable. She loved the subtle luminosity of the oil lamps filtered by shades and screens. It was a welcome change from the journey, after that excessive glare and exposure to the elements.

The lieutenant informed her, however, that it was a provisional arrangement, since he was expecting the arrival, any day, of a European mistress, who would be coming by coach from Buenos Aires. The idea seemed preposterous but it was true. A number of the officers already had such companions, and Ema wondered what exorbitant sums must have been offered to persuade these courtesans to renounce the world and come to the frontier. They never showed themselves, and all the news of them was gleaned from their maids.

The officers organized their time in a defiantly unnatural manner. They burned sandalwood and slept drunkenly on the damasked sofas; gambling was their sole occupation for months on end, either among themselves or with the chiefs who came to visit for that purpose. Softened by the gambling, they needed endless hours of sleep.

That was where she saw the Indians for the first time — Indians of a particular kind, since only the grandest chiefs came into the fort, always with exorbitant pomp.

One night, not long after her arrival, one of the other women came to find her and said that two wealthy princes had arrived and were gambling with the officers in the salon. Ema asked if it would be possible to see them.

"Yes. But don't make any noise. They don't like to be distracted."

They went out onto the balcony holding hands, and approached the rail on tiptoe; it was barely visible against the feeble illumination from below, where a single porcelain lamp was alight at one corner of the rug on which the men were playing.

The furniture had been pushed back against the wall. It was hard for Ema to make out the scene, because of the darkness and the positions of the players, but also because of the perspective: she was looking down almost vertically.

Among the faint gleams that streaked the darkness, she could see two indigenous gentlemen, painted from head to toe, their heads shaved at the front with very long, oiled hair growing at the back. Behind them, also sitting on the floor, were other Indians, who were merely observing, their cigarettes held by beautiful kamuros, who were painted too but with black ink, which made their small, graceful bodies disappear into the shadows. And the officers, all in their ornate dress uniforms with gilded buttons, wreathed in tobacco smoke. The crisp and multiple clicking of the dice on the boards was the only sound; it seemed to hang in the silence.

It was a magnificent sight, and Ema would never forget it.

Later, in the course of the month and a half that she remained there, she witnessed many such gatherings, and even attended some, keeping a certain distance. She observed the indecisive movements of the Indian women, and let their passionate spirit flow into her. On gambling nights they lit only one lamp, with the weakest flame; that dimness recreated the conditions of the forest at night. The limbs of the Indians seemed red, like fiery copper, and the charms tattooed on the women's skin became nets in which the darkness quivered.

They drank continually. The fort provided the finest liqueurs, which were served out by the women. Sometimes, after many hours of gambling, they realized that, since the beginning, they had been hearing a continuous flowing sound, as if they had been on the banks of a river, but it was just the sound of the cups being filled.

It was most unusual for the officers to turn in before dawn, and they would often stay at the gaming rug for days and nights on end. That too was something Ema enjoyed. She liked to see the morning light filtering in through the closed shutters, while the gambling continued inside, and the men pursued their nocturnal occupations with a drunken stubbornness, in spite of all the evidence, and the bugle sounded for the day's first change of guard, muffled by heavy upholstered doors and double or triple walls, summoning some officer, who would pick up his bundles of cash without a word and stagger away.

The spring nights tended to be rainy. Ema had never seen

such storms. Lightning flashes filled the sky, and thunderclaps came one after another, or simultaneously, for hours on end. If the women were alone, as usual, they would go out onto one of the covered balconies on the second floor and watch the storm in silence, smoking ... The agitation of the elements contrasted ideally with the players inside who barely moved all night. Sometimes, before the women decided to return to their rooms, an unidentifiable shadow (an officer who had run out of credit, perhaps, or a ghost), would join them at the back of the balcony, beyond the reach of the lightning's glow, and disappear again without introducing himself.

Finally, Paz's European mistress arrived, with two carts full of luggage and three maids. As soon as he received the news that she had reached Azul, Paz went to the village to arrange Ema's accommodation. He found a soldier who wanted a wife, a certain Gombo (obviously a false name, but almost all the men had a past that they were anxious to leave behind). The girl gathered up her few belongings, received the officer's gift of a Cossack pony and left with Francisco. When the gaucho set eyes on her, he seemed to be disappointed: too girlish, too immature. When it came to women, the troops did not share the officers' artificial tastes; their desires were coarser.

But he kept his word, and even evicted his two Indian concubines so that she would feel more at ease.

Gombo was a conscript, like the rest of them. He had been on the frontier for more than ten years, enduring all the vicissitudes of melancholy. Affable by nature, kindhearted, and almost excessively polite. Besides gambling, he loved fishing. Although he was not yet forty, his drawn, ascetic face was deeply wrinkled, and his hair was going gray. A while back, he had been promoted to corporal and then demoted for some reason. None of which mattered to him in the least.

They didn't spend much time together. When he wasn't on sentry duty at the fort, Gombo went fishing for days and nights on end in far-off places, or got together with his friends to gamble. So Ema had long days of solitude in which to grow accustomed to her new life.

The hut faced onto the single curving street of the embryonic village. The dwellings, all about thirty yards apart, were small and fragile, raised on piles, with square wooden verandas. There was nothing serious about them: they were frivolous, toys made of bark and paper. In the case of an attack, everyone would have to take refuge in the fort, and leave their little houses at the mercy of the savages. The street ran around the base of a hill, which provided some protection from the south winds. Plants grew quickly there, so quickly that some huts were already disappearing into the foliage.

The white population of Pringles was made up entirely of the soldiers and their women. Real colonization would not begin for many years to come. Peace with the Indians was extremely difficult and fragile in Azul; three hundred miles further out, in Pringles, it was not even on the agenda.

This was the first time Ema was able to observe the Indians in less formal circumstances. And since she had nothing else to do, her knowledge of their civilization grew considerably. On the other side of the hill, along a tributary of the Pillahuinco river, there was a large settlement of so-called tame Indians, who lived under the protection of the fort, though no one really understood the basis of the relationship. Their feather-light tents, of scant practical use, stood here and there on the steepest parts of the bank. They drank and gambled with the soldiers, or went fishing and hunting, or simply looked for pleasant spots to spend the afternoon. The soldiers were always invited to their tribal ceremonies.

As luck would have it, the first night that Ema spent outside the fort was the night of the Monkey Festival. Carrying her sleeping child, she set off with Gombo to find a place on the beach. All the village women were there, and the soldiers, and various officers, who had come out of curiosity.

There was no moon. People were scattered about at random on the grass. The only light came from fires in which aromatic substances were burning. The figures seemed to be barely sketched in, distinguished from the shadows only by their movements. While waiting, the people drank and smoked. All the Indians were painted. The children ran around everywhere, playing; no one tried to stop them.

In a large wicker cage hanging from a low branch was a little female monkey. Ema didn't see her until much later on, because she was beyond the firelight's range. The animal seemed to be asleep. A child, in the course of his running about, thrust the cage aside; then a man got up and stopped it swinging.

That was the ceremony: nothing, in other words. The adults kept still and quiet the whole time. The ritual was simply an arrangement, meagre and ephemeral, something that required a maximum of attention while rendering attention futile. Leaving after midnight, Ema made no attempt to hide her disappointment.

Gombo smiled and said nothing.

All the Indian ceremonies that Ema would attend later on were the same; they all celebrated a supreme inconclusiveness… Supreme because the conclusion was not even withheld: at a certain point the ceremony was simply over, and all the people went back the way they had come.

THE RAIN LASTED ALL NIGHT AND CONTINUED FEEBLY into the morning. In the hesitant dawn, a slanting ray of sunlight produced a rainbow, which was soon effaced by a wash of luminous gray. The birds announced their presence, one after another: the inhuman screeching of the flamingos was followed by the swallows' twittering, then the language of the lapwing, which sometimes seemed to be saying "lapwing," and finally by the resonant caw of a crow in the forest. The murmuring of the water was an invitation to sleep: Ema would have slept a while longer, but a movement in the shadows woke her. It was the little Indian girls, playing and laughing under the sheets. When she opened the shutters, they ran all around the hut. Francisco was sleeping: nothing would wake him until he was hungry.

The girls offered to go and fetch the milk. But wouldn't they get wet? They didn't mind the rain. Ema gave them a jug and a handful of bills so that they could buy cakes if the store was open. She always had a good supply of Espina's money in her hut: there was no knowing when it might come in useful. She found her two parasols and gave them to the girls. They ran off like does, leaving Ema on the veranda contemplating the desolate spectacle of a puddled street and the trees weighed down with water, heavy as blocks of stone. Black-faced ibis flew over, croaking among the threatening clouds.

Sitting in the rocking chair, half asleep, Ema lit one of the cigarettes the girls had left behind (they had been smoking since early childhood, accustomed to it by their mothers). The cigarettes were short and fairly thick, made with extremely fine paper and hollow cardboard filters. When she smoked on an empty stomach, they made her dizzy. She had the impression that time was standing still, except at the cigarette's burning tip.

Very soon the girls came running back. As well as the milk and the cakes, they brought eggs, bars of cocoa, pies, and a basket of wild plums. They announced, in reedy, quavering voices, that they would prepare breakfast. They were drenched and left wet footprints on the mats. Ema let them take care of it all; from the veranda, she could hear them moving about and chattering. Soon they came out carrying trays laden with steaming bowls.

When the baby woke up, they fed him milk through a straw. He looked at the gray day with dull eyes—the remains of the rain were still hanging in the air—and sucked hard.

They were finishing breakfast when one of the neighbors appeared, a stocky "soldier woman" with African blood; the slightest effort always made her go red. She wore spectacles thick as magnifying glasses, with frames that had been broken and mended; they were always slipping down her nose. She came running from her hut, trying to avoid the puddles, but unluckily stepped in every one and ended up soaking herself. Panting and shaking her parasol, she climbed up onto the veranda where Ema and the girls were sitting. They brought her a folding chair, onto which she collapsed, and offered her doughnuts.

"I need to catch my breath first, hhuh, hhuh."

She seemed to be about to choke. The girls stared at her. But when she recovered, she ate and drank more than the rest of them put together. Her husband was asleep—he'd been up all night drinking—and her children were playing in the muddy street. She had four boys, with four different fathers, all myopic like her.

"How long's the rain going to last?" she asked. "Autumn begins tomorrow. The wet weather is so sad. This will be your first winter here, won't it?"

Ema nodded.

From the fort came the sound of the seven o'clock gong. It had stopped raining. The sky was silvery. The two women rolled cigarettes. They were smoking and watching the girls, who had gone down into the street, when suddenly they heard the hoofbeats of a horse. Because of the way the street curved, the couldn't see the animal, which took its time as if going from hut to hut, and finally appeared at the bend. The rider was a soldier known to them both, without a kepi, his wet fringe stuck to his forehead. When he saw them, he stopped dawdling and steered his big white colt in their direction, bringing it right up to the veranda.

"A good morning to the early risers."

"What could possibly have got you up at this hour?"

"Colonel's orders," said the soldier. "An urgent summons."

That was unusual. They were expecting him to say something more, but all he did was look at them.

"In that case," said Ema's neighbor, "I'll have to wake my husband."

"He better hurry. They have to report for duty in half an hour."

"Why?"

The soldier shrugged his shoulders. With a gesture, Ema prompted the girls to hand him a cigarette, which he lit himself.

"What's it about?" the women asked him. "You must have heard something."

"I shouldn't say, but ... Apparently the colonel's worried about a raid."

"A raid?"

"That's right. A raid."

The neighbor overdid her shocked expression.

"But how could he know? Unless he can see into the future."

The soldier looked at her coldly and said nothing. She went mumbling back to her hut, leaving her parasol behind. Ema, for her part, was puzzled. The soldier watched her through the smoke of his cigarette.

"Will we have be to shut in the fort as well?"

"If that's what the colonel orders. Who knows? Maybe the Indians are still far away."

He tossed the cigarette away and rode off toward the last huts in the street.

Ema sent her little friends back to their camp, asking them to come and tell her if there were any new developments. The news had set the whole village in motion, and now the street was seething with activity. Half-dressed soldiers with puffy eyes came out of the huts and saddled their horses. Carrying her child, Ema joined a huddle of neighbors. It was the first scare since her arrival. Traditionally, the Indians did not attack during summer. Perhaps this time they wanted to celebrate the start of autumn with some pillaging. According to some of the women, on several occasions they had been under siege in the fort for weeks on end: an unpleasant prospect for Ema, who had grown accustomed to her excursions.

Soon they exhausted their speculations and the group broke up. It had begun to drizzle again. Ema went to have coffee with a neighbor, a young half-Chinese woman, who had three children and was heavily pregnant.

"When are you due?"

"In the next few days, any time now."

"It'll be hard for you if they make us go to the fort."

The neighbor shrugged.

"Makes no difference to me. I'm convinced it's all a trick, anyway. Who knows what Espina's up to, but I bet the Indians have nothing to do with it."

The inside of her hut was odd, with tiny red chairs, a bougainvillea in a blue pot, and a row of stuffed herons. The two women spent the morning chatting and smoking, while Francisco played with the neighbor's children. Just before midday an Indian girl came looking for Ema: the savages had appeared in the distance, on the other side of the river. Ema and her neighbor went outside immediately and joined the procession of women climbing the hill. There was some surprise that the colonel had not decided to give the population refuge in the fort. They supposed that he would do battle on the plain.

"And what if he can't stop them?"

One way or another, they all suspected that something strange was going on, something not entirely real.

When they came to the top of the hill, only those with the sharpest eyes could see, on the horizon, beneath the mists left by the rain, the insect-like figures of the Indians' advance guard. Officers with telescopes crowded the fort's little towers, and occasionally a spot of sunlight reflected off a lens would flitter through the crowd like a moth. The children played excitedly and kept running off, in spite of their mothers' warnings.

The figures got bigger very quickly. According to a rumor, the colonel had proposed a meeting of ambassadors. Whether this was true or not, the onlookers were sure that they would witness negotiations rather than combat. The column of Indians came to a halt, and a few leaders hesitantly went on ahead.

The doors of the fort opened. The colonel in person came out with an escort. Opportunities to see him were rare, since he generally stayed within the palisades. He was a burly man, with a big gray mustache that looked white because of the contrast with his dark skin. He was wearing a dress uniform and rode out on a powerful bay horse to meet the savages, who were approaching at walking pace on the other side of the river, their bodies painted red and gold, with blue feet and calves. The colonel and his men crossed at a place where the water was shallow over a slew of pebbles.

The two parties stopped a few yards apart. Espina was the first to speak. From the hill, his words were indistinct, although he spoke with a resonant voice. The Indians squinted at the ground and replied with coughs and monosyllables. The speeches went on for a long time, maintaining the suspense.

Ema turned and looked at the fort. The mistresses had appeared on the towers, wrapped in silk and tulle like chrysalids, their faces covered with iridescent makeup. They were rarely to be seen, although they did occasionally venture out to the forest in closed carriages.

The conversation had reached an impasse. The men were silent, the horses turning on the spot. Finally the colonel gave an order to the lieutenant, who went galloping back to the fort. Less than five minutes later (all of this had been prepared), he came out again, very slowly this time, in a silence so deep you could hear the crickets. Behind him came a voluminous cart pulled by two teams of oxen. The load, covered with tarpaulins, swayed as if it were about to topple. By this stage all the spectators were convinced that they were watching a performance. It must have been a kind of ransom in exchange for which the Indians would call off the imaginary raid. When the cart came to ford the stream, some curious onlookers, who were asked to help, managed to get a glimpse of the load, and that was how the rumor started: it was cash—bundles of bills, tightly packed. Many people remained skeptical, because of the colossal sum that such a cargo would represent.

But the handover dispelled their doubts: one of the Indians lifted a corner of a tarpaulin and poked around in the money with the point of his spear. Without saying anything more, he climbed into the driver's seat, and off they went, at a leisurely pace. The colonel returned to the fort like a breath released, the gates closed behind him, and it was all over. Laughter was heard.

Emma went down to the bank of the river, curious to hear what the Indians were saying. She took her place in a circle of young people who were drinking.

"I think the colonel has come up with the simplest system for avoiding wars," said one of them ironically. "Why didn't anyone think of it before?"

"Maybe it's not such a novel system," someone else put in. "Maybe it's what people have always done. Underneath the frills, history is just a series of payments, the more exorbitant the better. The form and the credit arrangements have changed, but that's all."

"And besides," said another, "there has never been a war. Which shows that they've always been able to put it off."

Everyone agreed.

"War is impossible, so the payments are always futile, or rather, fictitious, like the one today."

Another member of the group said that it hadn't been so fictitious: after all, they'd seen the money and it was for real.

The one who had spoken earlier burst out laughing.

"Real money! That's ridiculous! Money is an arbitrary construction, an element chosen purely for its effectiveness as a means of passing the time. Those bills were printed by the colonel; all he has to do, whenever he feels like it, is start up the new press built for him by the Frenchman." He remained thoughtful for a moment, then added: "I bet it was all carefully scripted in advance."

"But why would he stage such a childish comedy?" Ema asked.

"To get the money circulating; it's a bother to distribute otherwise. And it sets a precedent. Maybe, from now on, all conflicts will be like this: a comedy of extortion. A new model. If he gets all the tribes on the outer circuit involved, he could end up shifting several tons of paper money per week."

They all admired the colonel's boldness. But an Indian woman had her doubts.

"For the moment, all that money is in the hands of one or two chiefs, maybe even just Caful ..."

"It doesn't matter. The money won't be any use to Caful, or anyone, unless they find a way to distribute it. Or some of it, at least: enough to create a monetary 'climate.'"

"And what if the chiefs decide to spend it all among themselves, doing political deals?"

"That's the risk Espina's running. But I don't think it's likely. Sooner or later money always filters down from the rich to the poor."

Another one of the Indians, who had been listening in silence, shook his head.

"I'm not so sure about that. For a start, that fortune in the cart is all going to end up in one place: the gaming table. Within a few hours of getting it, they'll have spent the lot, down to the last cent."

"Maybe it won't be that easy. We don't know the denomination of the bills. Maybe there's no one in the whole desert who could meet the stakes. And anyhow, gambling's just a way to lubricate circulation. You could even say that it *is* circulation, in its most accelerated form."

"Circulation," the other retorted, "is based on continuity, while gambling produces reversals of fortune that are discontinuous by their very nature."

"Gamblers," another man said, "always end up losing everything, so there is a concentration, although it's negative. It can't be an effective way of distributing goods."

It was pointed out in reply that the savage kingdoms had based their finances on gambling ever since prehistoric times, and the system had not collapsed, which meant that it didn't work too badly. The Indians were always going back to prehistory; it was their favorite way of explaining things. In the midst of this discussion, a cadet appeared on the beach looking for Ema, and handed her a letter folded six times. Gombo was informing her that he would have to stay at the barracks that night and would not be able to leave until the next morning. She supposed that he had received a bonus after the recent events and wanted to stay in the fort to gamble it away.

When there was nothing left to say, the group broke up. Some acquaintances invited Ema to camp with them in the forest, and she accepted: it was a good day to get away, with a dull sun trapped among gray clouds and expectation in the air. They set off in a file for some solitary clearing, Ema on the croup of a big bay horse with the baby slung from her shoulder. For three or four hours, they followed chilly paths enveloped in greenish light. Finally, at a random spot, they dismounted, built a fire, bathed, and began to smoke and play dice. They roasted birds and drank themselves to sleep. As the sun was going down, they were woken by the noise of brawling hyperborean geese. They bathed again, went hunting woodcock and piglets for dinner, and then night fell: the days were growing shorter. They drank and smoked into the small hours, dropping off one by one.

When the sun came up, they returned. Ema went to her hut. After putting Francisco to bed, she prepared some coffee, whose aroma attracted a neighbor. The two women went on weaving their conjectures about the events of the previous day. Ema asked after her neighbor's husband.

"He couldn't leave the fort last night. They say the colonel has put them to work on the printing presses."

Later on, when they got bored, they went out into the garden: the rain had finally opened the anemones, which were all red and blue.

Gombo turned up at midday, in a daze of fatigue, with black bags under his eyes. He went straight to bed and chatted with Ema while she held his cigarette.

"Is it true that the colonel is going to make you all work on the printing presses?"

Gombo laughed hoarsely.

"That's absurd. Those machines don't need operators."

"So what explanation did they give you?"

"None. Why would they give us an explanation?"

"Everyone in the village has a theory."

"It is intriguing, I have to admit."

"What was the colonel hoping to achieve?"

"Espina isn't God, and he's not trying to play God either—he's not that stupid—except in the most superficial way. He began by creating money. Now it must be time for the second phase: creating the goods to spend it on. But he's not interested in that; he's bowing out. All he wants is to get the money circulating perfectly."

"So the attack came in handy ..."

"There was no attack. That was a bit of playacting; he rehearsed it the other day with Caful's nephews."

Ema pondered this. She spent the afternoon in the garden, basking in the sun with her child, and when Gombo woke up, after nightfall, she learned something new: in exchange for the "financial solution," the Indians had promised to send the colonel a gift of a hundred pheasants, his favorite delicacy.

And so it was. The next day the cart returned, transformed into a huge wicker cage, divided into various levels and compartments that contained a hundred plump and colorful pheasants. The whole village came to see them being taken into the fort, where the officers and their *cocottes* would dispose of them in a couple of dinners.

A FEW WEEKS PASSED, AND THE PAYMENT FAILED TO produce an instant transformation, which is to say that it produced no effect at all, since on the frontier the slightest delay suppressed any change in favor of eternal repetition. Apparently other deliveries were made, to other tribes, under cover of darkness; but no one could really be sure, not even the soldiers on guard. When night fell, everyone thought they could see carts loaded with money stealing away toward the forest. Discretion and mystery created an atmosphere of historical significance, to which no one was immune.

Just as a *void* can attract everything within its range, thought Espina, a space that is *overly full* can expel everything of value, or value itself, in the direction of a certain person or anyone at all.

The void is nature.

But how could the world be overly full? Fullness, by definition, is never excessive.

Money was Espina's answer, quantities of money. True, nothing can be overly full, but this applies only to concrete things. Excess is an epiphenomenon of monetary systems, and could hardly exist without immense and incommensurable quantities of money.

Such was the reasoning of this enigmatic printer of notes. The results of his operation were subjective. Suddenly, those remote and almost mythical Indians, the subjects of Catriel and Cafulcurá, the tributaries of the emperor Pincén, entered the sphere of daily imaginings, since they were all linked (or so it was supposed) by the bills that were circulating out there. And when the hototogisu sang at night, the settlers felt, for the first time, that its song, redolent of dealing and finance, mantled the one dream, shared by all. Espina was claiming Pringles's place in the sun (or on the moon). The marvelous dawn set the crammed space turning, and pressed it, secreting a drop of gold in the brain of its inventions. The vast Indian empire became homologous with an art of interpretation. Even for the least poetic of souls, the vision of immensity was transformed by the idea of humankind burning incense before colored papers covered with numbers, because the numbers had a meaning that exceeded the realm of the human.

The village was flooded with money. The wages of the soldiers had been multiplied by a hundred. Espina backed his currency with his stocks of Indian cash; the Indians, venturing into the absolute, issued their bills without any backing.

Could it have been true that the colonel was sending millions and millions in his new currency to England? It was not impossible. If his idea, from the start, had been to consider the savage empire as a limitless territory (savagery itself had no limit, as his own behavior showed), there was no reason why it shouldn't include an archipelago as distant as Great Britain. In any case, on the pound notes, he printed a portrait of the queen alongside his own.

Meanwhile, in the fort and the village, life went on as before. The days were long strips of leisure and distraction, and people were treated as a part of each day and its atmospheric beauty. The timbó trees went on producing their effect on the fish, as arrows did on the ducks; the sound of dice on the gaming board continued to resonate as before, and in the evenings the water kept the bodies of the swimmers afloat.

The Indians kept sending parties of emissaries. It seemed that they had much to discuss with the colonel.

Although the common people barely glimpsed the diplomats passing by on their way to the fort, where the talks were held, they could not fail to be impressed by their splendor and magnificence. They had assumed that when it came to frivolity, they had seen it all. But now they realized their mistake. They were seeing things of which they had never even dreamed. The colonels' bills had reached their far-flung addressees; now the replies were beginning to arrive, and being replies to money, they were necessarily sumptuous: infinite possibilities, reality entire, the treasure of the poor.

As time went by, the diplomatic visits became more numerous. The members of the entourage generally preferred not to enter the fort; they would wait for their masters in the fields, beside a stream that ran into the river, underneath the trees. All the inhabitants of the village and the local Indians came to see them, and the contact with the strangers would sometimes last for days on end. The time they spent drinking and smoking together felt like pure magic. These were moments of learning, of watching and imitating. At first it all seemed so artificial, the hosts didn't think they would ever dare to repeat what they had seen. But the novelty overcame them like an irresistible wave.

Two or three parties or more, from different places, were often present at the same time. In which case veritable tournaments of elegance would unfold before the astonished eyes of the villagers. They were coming to realize how much importance they had granted to the inner life. The Indians could give them lessons in asceticism, obliterating everything beyond appearances.

The men in particular, painted from head to foot, were so powerfully present, so solid and heavy, that their bodies left a deep impression long after they had gone. Their eyes were tiny and generally half closed. An observer at very close range would have seen their irises shining like polished black boot leather, and their pupils, by contrast, glinting like diamonds. Their eyebrows and lashes were plucked. They wore broad, malleable gold bracelets, to concentrate energy. Their arms and legs were tightly bound with strips of cotton. On their fingers, dozens of rings, which they would remove, as if they were gloves, for a specially effective throw of the dice. Later they would pick the rings up without looking and slip them back onto their oiled fingers, one by one.

But their finest jewels—as they said themselves—were their gestures. Sleepily, darkly, slowly, with a fine awkwardness, they would extend an immaculate arm, like the wing of a swan, to lift a cup, and open their mouths unhurriedly, at irregular intervals, to draw on the cigarettes held by the women, and stretch their thick cylindrical legs on the grass in search of a more comfortable position. Their movements were the supreme crown of elegance: each time they lifted a cup to their lips, the choir of angels burst into song. The tensing or relaxing of a muscle, the transient line of a vein, the superslow wave that rocked a powerful back and shoulders ... These were so many signs of wealth.

As for the body painting, it defied all explanation; it was external to painting itself. Perfunctoriness had been a key aesthetic value among the Indians for centuries. Now they imitated the effect of a moth's wing randomly scattering its dust, or the squirts of a sponge soaked in black ink and squeezed against the chest; a flimsy grid on a herculean body; a warrior with blue arms; another hastily daubed with a paint that cracked as it dried ...

There were many shaved and painted heads; the silver scalp was in fashion. The rest had slicked their horse-like manes with precious oils.

They were aware of the dazzling effect their performances had on the white women. They used the marvelous gambits of etiquette to keep them in suspense. Of course, they were only minor courtiers; the VIPs met with the colonel in his salon. And *their* behavior, rumor had it, was utterly different, incomparably more refined.

At dawn (in general, although it could happen at any other time), the doors of the fort, made of banana trunks, would swing open, and the chiefs would come out on their chubby colts, as if they were riding in their sleep. Everyone would try to catch a glimpse of them in the hazy light, although they were not at their best, with their paint all smeared and their shoulders drooping with fatigue. The orgy had drained them of all vitality, and it was time for them to leave.

Abruptly abandoning their glamor, the warriors would leap onto their horses, the chiefs being in no mood to wait. There was not even time to say goodbye. Sometimes they would leave rings behind, or a die.

The Indians always seemed to be in the calm state that follows a storm of thought. That was why they were worth observing: to learn how a human being can recover from an upheaval that has not taken place. In a civilization like theirs, wisdom was everything. Imitating them was like returning to the source. Elegance is a religious, perhaps even a mystical, quality. The aesthetics of polite society: an imperative departure from the human. Sex and love were everything. According to Espina, love began with banking. But the Indians kept still; their sole occupation was hanging from the blue air like bats.

Winter was approaching. Each night was a little longer than the last. The social life of the savages intensified. The cold made them sleepy, and they liked to fall asleep in the middle of their favorite activities. They practically lived by night, under the clear, icy autumn skies, shining with familiar constellations, which they could reproduce with threads when they played cat's cradle. It was the season of love. The Indian women set the tone, looking beautiful with their bead necklaces looped as many as a hundred times, their well-brushed hair, black lacy masks painted onto the skin around their eyes, and their lips impregnated with gloss. Seduction was everywhere: a uniform field of passion and concentration. It became difficult to distinguish anything precise.

The big lizards that had populated summer with their siestas began to emigrate, after covering the mossy stones with their eggs. The lightest of them spread their wings and flew away. But the rest were heavy, as big as iguanas and drenched with green sweat; they headed off briskly for the north of the province, to sun themselves on the backroads. They would not return.

One day, the song and the untidy flight of some gray birds heralded the first snowfall. The next morning, the fields and the domes of the forest were white, the sky looked like wet paper, and a marvelous silence stretched away in all directions. Carts left black tracks in the street. The children built snowmen and ran around yelling, crazy with joy. The character of the landscape changed entirely. The white accentuated the women's dark luminosity. The hunters, painted red and black, stood out in the still panoramas. And the blue of the soldiers' uniforms blinked in the snow, as if hesitating between obtrusiveness and invisibility.

The contemplation of the snows, of course, expanded leisure time. In the depths of the woods, fires were lit to warm groups of young people playing dice, or listening to the birds, or cuddling. The song of the cardinal passed into the languages of the whetted wind and journeyed all the way to the horizon. By night, the furtive call of the otter could be heard; and rabbits held the horses' totalizing gaze with their superquick capering.

A CALANDRA LARK LAUNCHED ITSELF FROM THE frosty hedge and flew effortfully to the eaves. The leaves crackled and broke, brittle as glass, under its claws as it walked. The cold had hardened all that was normally soft, including the lark's tongue. The bird produced two long, inarticulate sounds, and then tried a trill that came out as a few staccato notes and a sneeze. Its throat was frozen. This was no climate for a singer. The hut was giving off an aura unlike that of the trees. The lark needed complications to survive. It shook the ice crystals out of its wing feathers.

Ema heard the notes and slid back one of the white paper shutters to look. She had slept on a mat, covered with blankets. Gombo had left at dawn, and after breakfast she had lain down again. Pregnancy made her drowsy; she often slept for much of the day. Francisco was asleep in his crib, under a down quilt. From where she lay, Ema could see the sky through the open window. A uniform, shining gray.

It must have been early. It would snow again, no doubt. Perhaps the lark would decide to come in.

She was half asleep when she heard the child cry. A slight breeze, most unusual on a day of snow, shook the window papers, and then it was calm again.

After a while, since Francisco had woken up and was crawling all around the room, looking for his marbles, Ema got up to make him breakfast. She gave him a bronze spoon with which to play the xylophone. She heated up some milk and poured it into a cup, which he knocked over. In a sudden fit of frustration with his own clumsiness, he threw the marbles out the window and laughed. Then he drank his milk enthusiastically. His mother wiped his face and combed his hair. She folded the mats, washed the dishes, and looked out the window. The glass marbles seemed to be floating on the snow. The anemones were still flowering, in spite of the cold, preserved by the supernatural calm of the previous days.

The whiteness was excessive, perfect. It radiated even from the colors. The snow shone.

She turned around suddenly, feeling that someone was watching her. Dazzled by the brightness, all she could see were shadows, but there was someone in the doorway. The silhouette of an Indian stood out against the background of the snowy street. Francisco stopped playing and watched him silently. There was something in his hand: a flute.

He stepped inside and into the light from the window. He was a very slim young man, with small, almond-shaped eyes, barely open, like slits over his prominent cheekbones, and indistinct black painting on his arms. He looked at her blankly.

Ema turned toward the stove and asked him if he wanted coffee.

"Sure," he said.

He sat down and cradled Francisco in his arms. The child could not stop playing with the man's superb black hair. All that brushing with oil gave the Indians' hair a consistency unlike anything except the most diaphanous water.

"I didn't think you'd come today," said Ema, bringing two coffee cups to the table.

"Why not? It's a perfect day to go to the forest and see the snow. You can't stay shut up in here."

Ema shrugged.

"I'm so sleepy all the time."

"You can sleep in the forest. We can spend the day there … When is your husband getting back?"

"The day after tomorrow."

"Then we can go to a place far away, where you've never been, and fish, and stay for two nights. There's bound to be a lot of snow; you'll be surprised."

"Is it very far?"

He gestured vaguely in the direction of the Pillahuinco, and since Ema had rolled him a cigarette, he put Francisco on the ground and took a couple of puffs. Then he went to get the horses, and they agreed to meet at the edge of the village.

Ema dressed the child warmly and picked him up. Carrying a few things in a wicker box slung over her shoulder, she walked through the snow, in the midst of an absolute stillness, to the hill. Not a single birdcall: the fine leaves of the baccharis emerged from the mass of snow, the surface of which was broken here and there by the tracks of a horse or a chicken.

She encountered no one on the way. On the hill she saw Mampucumapuro riding a little white mare and leading a big gray horse. A month earlier, in spite of her advanced pregnancy, Ema had begun a relationship with this young Indian, whom she had met on one of her excursions to the forest. When her husband was on guard duty, they would spend whole days and nights by the river. All they did was let the time go by. Winter was a very calm spell.

He helped her to mount the horse and hung a little canvas seat from one side of the saddle for the child. They set off at walking pace, the hooves of the animals crunching in the snow. Instead of entering the forest immediately, they set off across a field beside it. Finally Mampucumapuro pointed to a barely visible path, and they headed in that direction.

"I've never come this way," said Ema, and the sound of her own voice startled her.

"I know."

"It's absolutely quiet."

He took out his flute and played a melody. It seemed to be the only sound emanating from the world. Ema was nodding, letting her eyes close, when she was startled by the sudden flight of a bird.

"A water pheasant," said the Indian.

"I would have liked to see it."

A while later there was a noise among the branches.

"It's the mice."

"I thought they spent winter down under the roots."

"There's a species that prefers the cold."

When they reached the river, they saw a stone bridge. On the other side, they crossed an area of open ground. Trees appeared before them like ghosts.

"The snow makes everything seem different," said Ema.

"It's different," said Mampucumapuro, laughing, "because we're so far away."

"I've never come this far."

Mampucumapuro pointed toward the west.

"There's a village ten leagues in that direction. But we won't have to go that far. We're going to camp in a clearing I know."

When they reached the clearing, a precinct of snow surrounded by cypresses, Ema sensed a crystallized distance. The space was circular, and its silence preserved everything from disintegration, even randomly spoken words. Something on the ground caught her eye: a crushed parrot, wafer-thin, as if an enormous weight had pressed down on it. Those clean and brilliant colors against the snow made it one of the strangest things she had ever seen.

A natural tower of rock rose above the river, with a spiral of worn steps and a terrace at the top, from which there was a splendid view: scattered blocks of ice in the water, and beyond that a plain stretching away further than the eye could see. When they swept away the snow, the original slabs of rock appeared, with paintings, and the traces of innumerable fires. Mampucumapuro had brought a bunch of dry branches, which he lit; later, he said, he'd go looking for firewood. But first, he was going for a swim.

Watched by Ema, who was worried about the sharp blocks

of ice in the water, he went down to an overhanging rock and dived in. A few seconds later he reappeared, a little further out, clasping a trunk of transparent ice. He swam vigorously against the current up to the bend, let himself drift back, and repeated the exercise several times before getting out of the water. He came back blue with cold and dripped on Ema and Francisco. He sat very close to the fire, as if he wanted to embrace the flames, and the water began to evaporate from his skin. Ema wrung his hair dry, down to the last drop, then plaited it.

"All your painting has come off," she said.

It was true: his arms were clean.

"I'll redo it later on, and better. On the bank I saw little black berries, the ones that have the best pigment."

He was especially fond of black body paint, just as others preferred red or gold. He would quite frequently stain himself black from head to foot.

They unfolded a board and began to play dice. Chance, as always, revealed itself with a special intensity. It was as if each throw of the dice contained an enigma to be deciphered by the next throw, which contained an enigma in turn. It was a continuous, eternal game, the Indians' favorite. They used about fifty dice, so small they could all be held in one hand, with unique figures on every face, which made a total of three hundred different miniatures. At first it seemed too complicated, but with a little practice it became so easy you could see why it was called "the daydreamer's game."

They had to keep an eye on Francisco, who like all children

was irresistibly drawn to the dice. Mampucumapuro had a beautiful set, made of hard wood with enameled designs.

"My older daughter got hold of them one day," he said, "and scattered them, but I was able to find them all, except for one, which I had to make again."

He rummaged through them with a fingertip and picked one out. On its faces were a tree, a snail, a window, a martin, a cloth, and a crumpled pointy hat.

"Did you do the painting yourself?"

"Except for the cloth. A simple design is the hardest of all for the amateur miniaturist. One little careless mistake and it could be a picture of anything. The solution would be to turn it into something really difficult, but then it would be beyond me."

They played for a few hours, until they felt hungry. Mampucumapuro picked up his bow and arrows and looked into the forest.

"I'll be right back," he said.

He went off stepping carefully on the snow and disappeared into the trees. Left alone, Ema stoked the fire with a ball of resin. The silence was complete. She wondered if he'd be able to find any game: the world seemed so mute and deserted. Francisco played, throwing handfuls of snow into the fire. Ema rubbed oil into his hands. An owl flew past very low, with watery movements. She heard Mampucumapuro's steps; he was coming back. He had barely been gone a second, it seemed. Several fat birds and a bag of eggs were hanging from his belt. They plucked the birds, stuffed them with the eggs and some herbs, sprinkled them with cognac, and put them on to roast. Soon a delicious aroma was rising from the fire.

"Are they charatas?"

"Maybe. They were asleep, with their eyes open."

With some of the feathers, Mampucumapuro made darts to amuse Francisco. He doused the charatas with liquor again, which made the fire hiss, and finally removed them from the spits. All three ate enthusiastically.

Mampucumapuro promised to make more of an effort with the evening meal (the little birds had lacked flavor, he felt) and fell asleep smoking a cigar that Ema held for him. Then she fell asleep as well, with Francisco curled up against her chest, and when they woke up, the light had changed; it was more civilized, and the sky was a deep, dark silver color. They stoked the fire, which was going out. They played dice again while drinking coffee, then talked. Mampucumapuro played his flute; they invented amusements for the child. That afternoon marked a high point in their romance. It seemed immensely long. But they could see its end approaching. Emma crushed the little paper teacups and tossed them into the water. Dusk declared itself with opulent colors. A violet ceiling of clouds that lasted and lasted. Francisco had fallen asleep, and the lovers, in each other's arms, gazed into the strange, incomprehensible distances, waiting for something sublime that there was no need to wait for, since it was happening continually, without any kind of display.

In the last of the light, Mampucumapuro set off to get something for dinner. He returned with birds, freshly cut palm hearts, and a little peccary that he had found whimpering on a floating island of wisteria in the river, too scared to swim. Soon darkness fell.

Around midnight they heard noises. They were playing dice by the light of the fire. The moon had not yet risen, although, in its usual leisurely way, it was already spreading a glow from below the horizon. They couldn't see anything — Mampucumapuro guessed that the noise was a deer — but they must have been clearly visible themselves. Finally, youthful voices called out:

"Hey! Hey, dice-players!"

A party on horseback approached the tower, and made a commotion at its base. Ema and Mampucumapuro watched the strangers climb the stone steps and appear in the golden circle of firelight: several young people of both sexes, from an unknown tribe, who greeted them with bows and asked permission to warm themselves.

"Of course," said Mampucumapuro. "Come and sit with us. Where are you from?"

One pointed westward.

"Are you subjects of Caful?"

They didn't even know who he was. They came from much further away.

When the strangers discovered that Mampucumapuro and Ema were from Pringles (and that Ema was white, a detail that wasn't necessarily obvious at first glance), their interest grew. It struck her as odd that something as utterly mundane as the eastern edge of the Indian world could arouse curiosity. But perhaps it wasn't odd, just another confirmation of the world's enormous size, and the movement of time, which put humanity into perspective.

The newcomers settled down confidently by the fire, their body painting faded, barely visible, as if they had ridden in the rain. But enough of it remained to show that the designs had been extremely elaborate. They had brought a considerable amount to drink, and the first thing they did was propose a toast to the encounter. The women started rolling cigarettes. These were clearly not the sort of people who sleep at night. They seemed very alert. They were so aesthetic, or such aesthetes, that Ema felt they lent themselves too easily to parody. It must have been deliberate. They took out instruments: triangular harps the size of a hand, slide whistles that sounded like froglets, and little bark trumpets. To them, Mampucumapuro's flute with its thirty-six keys must have seemed clunky and outmoded.

The Indian women admired Francisco. A few of them were pregnant like Ema, and joked with her. Everything related to childbearing made them laugh—in their abstracted and melancholic civilization, birth was hilarious.

Later they played dice, which provided another kind of music. The snow, with its unique acoustic qualities, gave a special resonance to the sharp little sound of the dice on the board, and the blocks of ice colliding, and the voices of the Indians asking over and over: Are you asleep?

A ritual question, posed in a special voice, as dry as the whispering of reeds. Repeated again and again, like birdsong in a thicket.

By dawn the snow had stopped falling. The Indians drank boiling hot coffee and roasted little turkey hens. The men wanted to go swimming to wash off all the body paint before decorating themselves again. So they dived in with pumice stones and rubbed themselves until they were blank. They swam, pushing aside shells of ice and frozen tuna. When they got out, the sun was already beginning to rise, as white and silent as the world it illuminated. The women had made coffee and tea, and the men huddled together by the fire with their cups, laughing uncontrollably.

Once they were dry, they went to gather berries with which to stain themselves, and since these were berries of the finest quality, they stocked up. They crushed and boiled them to make a thick ink, which was best applied when still warm. They painted themselves with their fingers, disdaining the conventional brushes and straws, with rapid gestures and absent gazes, as if the resulting patterns made no difference and all they wanted was to get the task done. They painted Mampucumapuro too, and Ema: a discreet circle around her navel, which had been effaced by the distension of her belly. They threw what was left of the paint into the water: soft black arrows that trembled as they sank.

Wearied by the work, they smoked for a while, admiring each other.

"It's time to go," they said.

It seemed that they had important business somewhere, although they didn't say what it was. They whistled up their horses, who were nibbling at mushrooms among the trees, and took their leave flamboyantly.

"We leave you these bottles as a memento, so you can drink to our health."

"We will."

"Goodbye. See you."

Left alone, Mampucumapuro, Ema and the child suddenly felt exhausted. Their guests had worn them out with their superhuman refinement. They needed this silence. They drank and smoked for a while and, when they began to feel drowsy, rubbed themselves with resin in case it snowed. Soon they were asleep.

They woke up well into the afternoon. It had snowed, and the three of them were surrounded by the most immaculate white; the Indian's outstretched body, painted and oiled, seemed a sleeping incarnation of all the savage splendors. For a moment after opening her eyes, Ema didn't recognize him; she looked around at the white sky and the white crowns of the trees. The river was murmuring. She breathed deeply and felt the icy air rush into her lungs.

When Mampucumapuro woke up, he put a few armfuls of wood on the fire, picked up his bow and went hunting. He was back soon, as before, this time with an unbeatable catch: a ninety-pound duck, with red circles on its golden-brown plumage. He had shot an arrow through its neck.

They dined before the sunset's barbaric spectacle. As always at those latitudes, dusk brought together unrelated cosmic phenomena. And even though it was snowing, half the sky was a dark blue. Great bolts of lightning reclined on the horizon, beneath a fantastic rainbow. The stars grew, and a snowy moon rose over the white trees.

"At this time of day," said the Indian, "everything blends and is reconciled, as in a picture."

Ema was cutting pieces from the duck's breast for Francisco.

"A picture?"

"The world represents the brevity of life, the insignificance of humans." He made a sweeping gesture with the wing he was holding. "The fleetingness of life is eternal."

They tossed the bones into the river. In the distance they could hear the flamingos' cry announcing nightfall. They set off back to Pringles.

"WILL ESPINA'S PEACE LAST A THOUSAND YEARS?"
Gombo asked himself one night.

A pink paper lamp was shining in the middle of the room, and each time a gust of wind got in and made the flame flicker, the darkness in the corners jumped around amusingly, or the glow rose to the ceiling and lit up a golden fiber in the straw.

Freshly bathed and naked in his cot, Francisco laughed with half-closed eyes each time Gombo offered him a rattle. His bursts of drowsy laughter faded gradually until he fell asleep. Ema asked Gombo to stay there for a while or the child would start crying again. His little eyelids were turning pale. Gombo covered him and waited without moving. He was dressed in the white baggy trousers that he wore around the house and a starched white shirt. The kitchen fire kept the hut warm inside, but they could hear the wind blowing, laden with sleet and snow. A wild storm had broken at dusk, so they would be spending the evening on their own.

Gombo went to the table and poured himself a glass of wine from an opened bottle. He listened to the sounds of the wind and the thunder:

"It'll be worse for them up there," he said, pointing in the direction of the fort.

"Do they mount a guard when there's a storm?"

"In theory. But those towers are really flimsy, so the watch-men climb down and sleep at the base of them as soon as it begins to snow."

They remained silent for a while. Ema was working over by the kitchen. Gombo offered to light another lamp for her. They had a shelf full of them, all made of paper, and all broken in some way; they used them for going out at night.

"There's no need. I've nearly finished."

"What's that I can smell? A duck?"

"No, it's a guinea fowl. I bought it this afternoon from a man who was going past on a tall horse, a hunter."

"He must have been a trapper. Guinea fowl are easy game, easy money. Was he an Indian?"

"Yes, with black leaves tattooed on his chest."

What a pleasure conversation is, thought Gombo. They spoke of other things. A brown moth fluttered down from the ceiling. It was midnight. Ema got up again to take the bird out of the oven. The guinea fowl crackled in its gravy and gave off a swirl of golden vapor that enveloped her. With the utmost care she transferred it to a serving dish and poured the gravy into a bowl. Her husband was watching her, as always, with inexhaustible surprise. Although she was now on the point of giving birth, she had a mysterious agility. Everything was mys-terious, but no one ever spoke of that on the frontier. Besides, the guinea fowl was already on the table, and it looked deli-cious. Gombo had slept all day, so he hadn't eaten anything since breakfast. He made Ema sit down and went to get two clean glasses, then opened a bottle of champagne that he had won at dice, muffling the pop with a handkerchief so as not to wake Francisco. The lamplight had gradually weakened to a pleasant, dim yellow glow; the oven was still radiating warmth, although the fire was out; and, to accentuate the cosiness, the storm unleashed its full fury.

"I wouldn't be surprised if the wind swept up the hut and blew it to the other side of the forest," said Gombo.

He fetched a long, narrow knife and carved the bird expertly. The flesh was very soft. He gave Ema a wing, chose a drumstick for himself, and poured a spoonful of gravy over each piece.

They ate in silence, hearing all the noises of the storm renew themselves. The wind seemed to come and go, and there were gusts that crashed into the walls of the hut with a sound like thunder.

Ema ate just one piece of the fowl and drank a glass of wine; then she got up from the table.

"Don't you want any more? You should keep your strength up."

She shook her head and sat down in the rocking chair, at the edge of the lamplight, half closing her eyes. She put her hands on her belly.

"So restless!"

Gombo went over to feel for himself. She showed him where to place his hands, and he waited; eventually there was a big thump and a tumble, so unexpected that they burst out laughing.

"He's stretching as if he'd just woken up. Do you think he sleeps like we do?"

"He sleeps when you're asleep."

Gombo passed Ema an apple, which she nibbled halfheartedly, while he disposed of the rest of the guinea fowl and the bottle of wine. Then he leaned back in the chair and looked at her again. She had closed her eyes.

"Are you sleepy?"

"No, I don't think so. I slept all day."

Gombo produced a bottle of cognac and two glasses, which he warmed slightly over the candle before filling them. He took just a sip and got up again, to make the coffee.

"On a night like this," he said, "there's no rush to get to bed because you know that sooner or later you'll fall asleep anyway."

"Some people can't get to sleep when there's a storm."

"But we're not like that, are we? No one has trouble sleeping in Pringles. Sometimes I wonder … if sleep doesn't form a part of the landscape and the society we live in. But how could we quantify it?"

For a while he pondered this question. Ema had begun to roll two little cigarettes, and as her husband watched, captivated by the sure movements of her fingers, his meditation took a turn.

"Why is it …" he said in a dreamy voice, leaving the question incomplete.

Ema looked up.

"Why is it," he repeated, "that women roll men's cigarettes?"

Ema was accustomed to these interrogative epiphanies. Her husband seemed to have a gift for coming up with the most unexpected questions, distilling them from any situation, even the most trivial.

"Why, indeed?" she said, but he was too absorbed to notice her mocking tone, and simply repeated:

"Why?"

Ema slipped a rolled mulberry leaf into the lamp and used it to light the cigarettes. They began to smoke.

Gombo hadn't finished. After the first puff he went on talking.

"Just then, when I was looking at you, something occurred to me that actually has nothing to do with the cigarettes: why do pregnant women take up so much space? I don't understand."

"Space?"

"It's incomprehensible. What I mean is, they *become* space," said Gombo.

"They say that pregnant women are always seeing other pregnant women wherever they go. Does that answer your question?"

"No."

"Anyhow, there'd be no way to test it here."

"True. All the women are gestating. What else is there for them to do? At least it's a way of passing the time. Besides, that's why they've been sent to the desert. To populate it."

These were old Liberal jokes, which Gombo repeated out of habit, but his mind was elsewhere.

"When I said space, I meant something else. Where do children come from? When will the world be totally populated?"

"There are answers to all these questions."

"I know, my girl ... But ... sexual things are invisible. They don't show."

Gombo concluded with a vague gesture, wreathing himself in smoke. But the water was already boiling, so he slowly filtered the coffee. Its aroma made him chuckle: he had remembered something.

"My grandmother used to say: 'Nothing smells more gossipy than coffee.'"

They filled the cups and drank in silence. Then they poured themselves more cognac. The cigarettes had gone out; Ema rolled another two. How distant the storm was beginning to seem! And yet how close! All they had to do was reach out and touch it ... But they preferred not to.

"I wonder what happens to the storm in the forest."

It was usual to refer to the forest in this way: it changed everything.

"Nothing," said Gombo. "The storm doesn't exist in there; it can't get in. And even here, the forest is protecting us; on the plains, this house would be blown away. Hold on," he said when he saw that the cigarettes were ready.

He lifted up the lamp and removed the shade, a cylinder of paper hardened by the heat, which he left on the table. They smoked for a moment.

"In another place, we'd die out. But death is impossible here." He blew a column of smoke up into the air. "Totally impossible. Absolute protection." And he added: "Life is impossible, and death as well. Is there anything that isn't impossible?"

"It's possible to have children," said Ema.

"Very true. Now that I think of it ... the impossibility of life manifests itself differently in men and women, and perhaps in opposite ways. Maybe it's the only difference between them. And yet life is just as impossible for you as it is for me, or for him," he said, pointing at Francisco's cot. "It's all there is left. It's impossible for an individual to live within a species, or outside of one. It's not mysterious. On the contrary."

He paused (he was in the habit of pausing for a long time between one sentence and the next), and seemed to snap out of his philosophical mood. Pointing at Ema with his cigarette, he said, like a teacher to his pupil:

"If it weren't impossible, life would be horrific. You'd do well to keep that in mind. Maybe things will change in the future. Maybe life will be possible in a hundred years ... But luckily I won't live to see it."

There was a long silence.

"And yet ... our life dwells here with us, like a Finnish coach house in the middle of a snowstorm ... Life is always passing like a cloud, without touching anything or leaving a trace. Just like the storm: it leaves no trace because it repeats itself."

When Gombo spoke again, his voice was quieter and more shadowy, as if his thoughts had followed a long, secret path and reappeared very far away.

"In fact," he said, looking at the cigarette stub between his fingers, "We don't know what effect this might have on our bodies. The same with alcohol. If you ask me, we'll never know, no matter what progress science makes. It's like trying to know what time might hold in store for man ... the miniscule lapse of time between one heartbeat and the next. Chemistry creates time ... No, no ... it's gluttony. A man eats a mushroom: will he have sublime visions or die from poisoning? There's no way to know. Because of that detail we're condemned to ignorance of everything in the world."

Ema tossed the butt of her cigarette into the fire, and Gombo imitated her mechanically.

"Shall I roll another?"

He hesitated for a moment.

"One more, before going to sleep."

He watched her rolling a leaf that seemed to be pink. There was no thunder, but the whistling of the snow had grown higher and sharper. The whole village must have been asleep. Gombo poured himself a last glass of cognac (the bottle was almost empty) and leaned back on the chair, smoking in silence as Ema laid the mats on the floor ... Everything seemed to have become slower and quieter ... Gombo tapped the ash from his cigarette onto the plate with the bones ...

At that moment one of the walls of the hut tore from top to bottom like wet paper. A violent gust of wind extinguished their one lamp and transformed the warm atmosphere perfumed by cigarette smoke into a chaos of icy smells. The snow's nocturnal white was slathered with a fiery brilliance. The threatening silhouette of an Indian had appeared in the opening. As he prepared to enter, the torch he was carrying moved and illuminated his body, painted from head to foot with terrifying war patterns. His face was made up to look like a demon, but remained clearly visible. His head was shaven, and he was naked. Within a few seconds, the stunned couple realized that the

Indians had mounted a surprise attack on the village, under the cover of the storm.

Before the savage could step inside, Gombo leaped up, grabbed his sword from the chair on which it was hanging, and dealt him a powerful blow to the head, splitting it open. The stream of blood, dispersed by the wind, drenched them both. Ema was beside the cot; she lifted the child out, wrapped in blankets.

"To the fort!" shouted Gombo, over the noise of the storm, while the hut collapsed around them and returned to nothingness.

Although they could barely open their eyes, they glimpsed other Indians approaching. They ran along the anemone path. The storm was at the height of its fury; the snow was blowing in all directions, not just falling from above; sometimes great white blocks of it came away from the ground and crashed into their legs. The clouds flew past like eagles beneath the moon, and when an especially big one hid it entirely, the burning huts were the only source of light. Ema ran stooped over her son, Gombo with his saber aloft.

The nearest hut was blazing like a bonfire, and before they could get past it, they were intercepted by a group of horsemen, who seemed to spring right out of the flames. The high-pitched, inarticulate wailing they could hear came not from the Indians but their horses, who were mincing their tongues with their teeth and spitting jets of blood and foam. Ema just had time to see that the burdens they carried were unconscious women. One of the beasts knocked her down: she saw a night-mare head with eyes bulging from their sockets, all its hair on end, and swollen veins, thick as an arm. It bumped her in the dark, and that was enough to send her rolling over the snow. Her head was spinning, her body possessed by a furious alien movement. When she was finally able to rise to her knees, she was hidden by swirls of snow. She still had the child in her arms, but the blankets had blown away. She was alone.

It was hard for her to stand, heavily pregnant as she was. She remained on her knees for a moment, on the point of fainting. In that daze, all she could see were the chaotic coils of the blizzard. She thought she was staying still, but in fact the wind was dragging her along, as she realized when she collided slowly with a tree, a mulberry whose gnarled trunk provided shelter for a moment, although she was petrified by the whistling of its branches. She bent over Francisco and saw, in the glow of the lightning, that he was crying, although she couldn't hear him.

Suddenly, an even stronger blast of wind cleared the snow from the air, and for a moment she glimpsed the fort in the distance: silent and dark, bathed in moonlight, like a fantastic edifice erected on some dead planet. She saw Indians ride past with captive women slung over their horses, giving off a livid glow; the savages seemed like mannequins carved from darkness, tattooed with lines and circles. Since none of them had seen her, there was some hope; perhaps the attack was over, and they were going back.

The veils that made everything invisible were coming apart

and reforming elsewhere; suddenly they opened before Ema's eyes, and she could see a cottage a hundred yards away. Flames were rising from its little windows and had made its walls almost transparent; finally the roof exploded in a cloud of sparks.

The moon was hidden. The lightning revealed nothing but a tremendous confusion. The mulberry tree was shaking all the way down to its roots. Ema gave up hope: any moment they would go flying. She clasped her child more tightly.

The dark shape of a horseman loomed, very close; and then he began to approach, very slowly. In the midst of that frenzy, his calm was terrifying. She took him for a soldier, but only for a moment ... The whinnying of his horse dispelled that illusion. He must have been an Indian who had been left behind and was roaming the village, unable to resign himself to going back without a captive of his own. A ray of moonlight illuminated him: glistening with fat, head shaved, bands of sealing-wax red on his chest.

The moon had come out just to show Emma the savage's gaze. He came over and leaned down without dismounting, took her under the arms and seated her on the colt's neck. A moment later, the tree blew away.

Off they went. Ema's perspective changed. They passed burning huts; the fires were a very cold, bluish-violet color. Burning pieces of furniture flew over her head, contrasting beautifully with the black background of sky. With the help of a tailwind, the savage spurred his mount up the slope. At the top, he stopped for a moment; from there the fort was visible with its gates standing open, and the soldiers coming out and running blindly toward the village, holding their sabers aloft, like toy figures. He turned the horse around, and it galloped to catch up with the rest of the raiding party with its burden of women. They forded the river and plunged into the night, heading for the forest.

ON HIS ANNUAL SPRING EXCURSION TO THE ISLAND OF Carhué, the prince took an enormous retinue, almost three times bigger than was normal for such a trip, including musicians, assistants, masseurs, hunters, bodyguards and a huge number of children, as well as the multitude of hangers-on whose sole functions at court were to sleep and display their splendid headdresses, adjusted to suit the time of day and the circumstances. Against his father's advice, he had even insisted on bringing the white women given to him in recent weeks, with some of whom he hadn't yet had an opportunity to spend a night. The old chief's objections, set aside by his son with a disdainful smile, were rooted, if weakly, in traditional attitudes toward the island, a sacred refuge not to be sullied by the ambiguous presence of white people. It was understandable that Hual paid little heed to his father's opinion, since the island had been losing its holy character for decades and becoming the desert's most fashionable resort, the place where the richest chiefs gathered in summer, not in search of any kind of magical protection but merely to soak up the ambience of luxury and ease, and to indulge in more sensual pleasures. Nevertheless, all unawares, the prince was revealing remnants of the archaic disposition to nomadism by insisting on taking all the trappings of

everyday life, however much it complicated the trip. He wanted
to travel undiminished in body and soul. Watching him prepare to go on vacation with such a crowd, people predicted
that he wouldn't get much rest, but in the end these criticisms
came to nothing more than a shrug of the shoulders. After all,
if a wealthy minor chief wanted to travel in the company of all
his minions, or transport every last one of his greyhounds and
parrots hundreds of miles for a stay of a few weeks, just so he
wouldn't feel homesick, that was his prerogative.

A few days beforehand, a party of young men had set out
with the portable dwellings which they would erect on the island. Hual gave them many instructions, and a mass of drawings and diagrams specifying his requirements: not just the
dimensions and forms of the tents, but also their orientation,
their distance from the coast, and a thousand other details.

"Dear Hual," said one of his captains, without hiding his
irony, "if we were to take all this rigmarole seriously, we would
have to spend months setting up the shelters in which you want
to sleep a week from now."

"It doesn't matter. There'll be time."

They would have preferred to be guided by the moment's
inspiration, as usual. But Hual was stubbornly opposed to
chance; when he was seeing them off, it occurred to him that
perhaps they wouldn't be able to find the island, and he sent for
something from his tent.

"Take this map," he said.

It was a sheet of thick paper, folded into four and covered

with inscriptions on both sides. Sighing, they put it away with the rest of the luggage, and said, "Much appreciated."

Hual went on worrying, and repeated to anyone who would listen that the men were bound to get lost; when he arrived, there would be nowhere to sleep. He almost came to believe these fantasies, and at one point it seemed that he was about to give up the whole idea, but his fears were strenuously dispelled, and finally his party set out one day at dawn, with all the women, a reduced royal guard mounted on gray ponies, and a team of packhorses to carry their effects. The distance they had to cover was barely three miles, but they were taking so many children, and they stopped so often to drink, or take a siesta, or swim in each river they came to, that it took them five long days to get there. Hual was entirely relaxed about this. A tall man, with a well-proportioned, athletic body in spite of the utterly pampered life he led, he was very proud of his long black hair, always oiled and brushed, which hung down heavy as iron and hid half his back. His brutal features were redeemed by his eyes, which gleamed with a marvelous intelligence. His generosity was legendary. His peculiar neurosis consisted of approving every suggestion that was made to him. It was said, however, that in his youth, he had been a sadist. He looked about forty, although he was probably ten years younger.

On the fifth day of the trip, just before nightfall, they arrived at the lake's southern shore. Two of the scouts were the first to see it; they came galloping back along the trail to announce the good news to the prince and prevent him from calling an

ill-timed halt. Suddenly the forest opened out, and there was
a chorus of exclamations. In the gray light of the evening they
beheld a vast, smooth beach covered with birds. The water
stretched away as far as the eye could see. They had hoped to
be able to glimpse the island, but in the distance there were
only dark mists, from which a tiny, dot-like bird would occasionally escape.

Fascinated by this motionless spectacle, they proceeded to
the shore. After consulting with his lieutenants, Hual decided
to leave the crossing until the following day. They took flares
from the saddlebags to communicate with the advance party
and fired them off without waiting for it to get dark. The replies came a few moments later, from the faraway, mist-hidden
island: five white flares, and a green one that went spiraling up
into the sky before falling into the water.

Hual had his men pitch him a tent in the middle of the
beach, and called for drinks and cigarettes. The process of dusk
was beginning, with a taut, bright gray. The air seemed to be
charged with electricity. The whole company lay down quietly
on the gritty sand, even the children.

The warriors were exhausted, they didn't know why. Overcome by somnolence, they smoked. Some drank themselves to
sleep. They should have gone hunting but they didn't feel up to
it, and no one was hungry.

The horses ambled about, bewildered. They took a few steps
and stopped to look at the ground, disconcerted by the sand.
They waded hoof-deep into the whitish water, but when they

tried to drink, they discovered that it was salty and spat it out. The gray of their coats caught the last of the fading light, giving them a ghostly appearance. In the end, they let themselves drop onto the sand, and shut their eyes to sleep.

The greyhounds went back to the forest, where they felt more at home, and lay down among the leaves. From there they watched Hual's lethargic retinue with phosphorescent eyes.

The air was oppressive, almost unbreathable. It was too hot, although it was only the beginning of September. In spite of their inactivity, the travellers were glistening with sweat. They thought it was because of the water's proximity. The darkness was gathering, and before it was fully night, a huge yellow moon rose and transfigured them. There was no need to light a fire, so they didn't. The last thing they saw in the daylight was a big, masked stork flying past in the direction of the forest.

They moved only to pour a drink or lift a cigarette to their lips. One by one, they fell asleep where they lay, stretched out on the sand. By midnight there was no one was left awake. The stillness and the silence were supernatural.

But before dawn, a wild storm broke. The prince's tent blew away like a piece of paper, huge trees were torn up by the gusts of a freak wind, and all the water in the lake seemed to rise from its bed in a threatening scroll. A torrent of rain poured down. Bundles of flashes, lightning bolts heavy as meteorites.

Even so, few woke to watch the storm, and those who did were barely interested. Most went on sleeping until the first light of day, by which time everything was calm again. They opened their eyes to a world transformed: trees uprooted and piled on the beach; the horses buried in sand, with only their sleeping heads exposed like sculptures. The force of the wind had sucked tons of silvery fish from the depths of the lake and scattered them everywhere.

The prince, who always took a massive dose of pills to get to sleep, was the last to regain consciousness, and the most surprised. Speechless, he gazed at the upturned trees, the men digging out the horses, and the fantastic shapes of the sand, so different from the blank platitude of the day before.

But then the sun announced its arrival with gorgeous reds, the birds sang as if nothing had happened, and the savages rose to their feet with their distinctive lofty affability, opulent and well disposed.

A gigantic rainbow spanned the island and the lake in its entirety. Mists streaked with cerulean blue, left over from the storm, were lifting. Someone claimed to have heard the song of the cachila pipit, which was particularly rare. The insects stridulated energetically, as if they had lost their relatives in the confusion of the night.

Not having dined before sleeping, the travelers were hungry, but some felt that it would be better not to lose any time. Hual overruled them equably: while the warriors busied themselves assembling the rafts, the women would cook the best of the fish and mussels cast ashore by the storm, and a choice of the birds that had fallen from the sky. So it was. When they smelled the delicious scent of the food, all the men dropped what they were doing, and even the prince put aside his air of stupefaction to gnaw at the heads of trout and eat wild plums.

The women and the children would travel on the rafts. The horses were fitted with round cork harnesses (no easy task) to help them swim alongside. The warriors would row behind in a folding punt, loaded with all the prince's chattels. And the prince himself would make the crossing in his bark skiff, with a single rower. When they pushed off, the children exploded with joy, which provoked a grumpy reaction from the prince, who resorted to laudanum and morphine.

The shore receded behind them. Gradually they were surrounded by mist. The shrieks of the children helped the company to stay together, but they lost all sense of direction. In any case, they were bound to be approaching the island, which was at the geometrical center of the lake. And indeed they were. What they heard first was the song of the birds, a tremendous din of chirping that shook the island day and night. Then some mysterious hammer blows.

Finally, they made out gray shadows in the whiteness, which at first they took for clouds. But they were trees: the island's magnificent leafy roof. The shapes looked far too big, but as the boats approached, the vast dimensions settled down, and in the end the boats cast up on a beach of fine sand where everything seemed microscopic.

The horses were the first ashore, then the warriors, who began the hard work of unloading. The children ran about giddily, screaming. The women looked around. Clearly they had missed the camp site, since they couldn't see any sign of tents.

When Hual, helped by two of his wives, disembarked, he couldn't hide his distress.

"Where could those idiots have got to? Who knows when we'll find them." He looked at the trees along the edge of the beach. "The gumbo limbos are in flower. Can't you smell them? I'm sleepy, and I want to hear some music before going to bed."

Indeed, his eyelids were red with sleepiness. But a glance at his men revealed that they were in no state to attend to him. The effort of unloading the bundles and steadying the punt, up to their waists in the water, had worn them out.

Before long, the young men of the advance party appeared from behind a mound on the beach. Hual could barely contain his impatience. They greeted him with the customary bows, looking happy and satisfied, and being accustomed to the prince's volatility, continued to smile as they listened to his gloomy reprimands.

"The tents are ready, on a calmer, better beach, less than two hundred yards from here."

"Take me there," said Hual.

They set off. The young men chattered on, delighted by every detail of the island. Hual interrupted them: How many chiefs had come?

"We didn't have much time to look around, and even less to socialize," they said, "but as of yesterday there were just three little court parties, and we think one of them left during the night."

They told him the names of the chiefs: figures of middling stature; one was related to Hual. In two months time, at the beginning of summer, the desert kings would begin to arrive and amuse themselves, gambling, signing treaties, and relaxing in the sun. Hual, who in spite of his wealth, had no political power at all, preferred to spend a month on the island in spring. All that political posturing, he said, was a sham; he preferred the more thoroughgoing frivolity of dissolute seclusion and amorous gatherings.

And yet he'd never been able to have the island to himself, since all year round, even in the lulls between the winter and summer seasons, idle chiefs kept turning up with their courts.

After a five-minute walk they reached the tents, which were the quintessence of fragility. They had the look of star-shaped shells, a form achieved by attaching sheets of paper to a frame of twisted and bound wicker. It was amazing that they had survived the storm. But they were cleverly located among the trees, and perhaps the wind had not been able to get a hold on them. All of them faced the water. An aroma of freshly rinsed lime trees came wafting down to that poetic ocher-and-yellow encampment. Behind the tents were three little ceremonial towers, surrounded by taquara flutes, each four yards long, on which to summon the spirits that were likely to be about.

Still under the influence of his narcotics, the prince saw nothing. Cloudy-eyed, he turned to one of his wives, instructed her to roll out his mat in the central tent and announced that he was going back to sleep—they should have a look around the area and, above all, take the children with them. Four of five of his wives went into the tent to hold his cigarettes and attend to him; the rest of the party, excited by the novelty of the surroundings, headed off in various directions, having hastily dumped their loads. The children were given permission to go absolutely wherever they liked.

It promised to be a perfect morning: the sun, although high, was still veiled in red, and Venus shone like a tiny white orange. A breeze was blowing, full of scents and charged with a rousing saltiness.

The island of Carhué was four or five leagues across, oval in shape, and it had a strange topography, a combination of peaks and troughs, which meant that all the paths constantly rose and fell. It was ringed by a broad belt of sandy beaches, lapped by the waters of the famous lake, which were almost always calm and, like a miniature sea, hosted an exceptional variety of fish. Many chiefs went there exclusively for the pleasure of fishing, and some had quite irresponsibly introduced the strangest species, which had thrived by multiplication or interbreeding.

As for the flora, there was nothing to match it anywhere in the forest's eastern sector. The nearly constant temperatures, the frequent rain and the rich tertiary soils combined to make the island a comprehensive showcase of the most curious and beautiful plants imaginable.

Even in the hottest months the weather remained bearable, which explained the influx of summer vacationers, who would have posed a threat to the environment had they been more active and less given to drinking. At first it was only chiefs who came, in order to converse with their peers, but they were soon joined by all kinds of snobs and money-printers. There were no permanent residents: much as all the visitors enjoyed spending a season on that little floating paradise, it would not have occurred to any of them to settle there for good. The mere thought of it made them nervous.

As Hual's people explored the island in various groups they came across numerous camps set up here and there on the beaches or in the groves by parties from other tribes. Circles of youths, enveloped in fragrant smoke and surrounded by empty bottles and gourds. And in the middle, a dice-board. All their chiefs asked of them was to be left in peace. Utterly idle, they had nothing to do but paint themselves and be sublime from morning until night.

Each encounter involved a long session of greetings and explanations; the newcomers were invited to join the circles and play. Their welcoming and inquisitive hosts offered to act as guides and organize parties for the evening. But these offers had to be declined, since Hual might have had something planned.

The birds made a tremendous din. In spite of which, the visitors spoke in whispers, as people nearly always do in forests. Little white foxes fled before them as they went; these were ornamental animals, not for hunting. Their flesh, it was said, had a soapy taste, like that of the southern screamer. They could be caught by tossing them little cakes. They had milk teeth.

One of Hual's groups crossed the island diagonally and came to a beach on the northern shore, where they could hear shouts and bursts of laughter. As they came through a curtain of vines, they saw a multitude of youths swimming and playing on the sand. Catching sight of the visitors, the young men called out greetings and invited them to come and have a drink.

A powerful figure stood out among them: tall, painted in black and gray, with a hard gaze and a resonant voice.

"Who did you come with?" he asked them.

They told him.

"Hual?" he replied, raising an eyebrow.

"Do you know him?"

He nodded, with a vague smile.

"I'll go and visit him."

Meanwhile, another contingent was weaving its way through the jungle, five or six warriors and as many girls, carrying nothing but paper cigarette cases and necklaces of opaque stones. They had decided to search for one of the island's famous springs, although they knew it would be hard to find. They trekked up a wooded hillside, not noticing the climb, until they heard the sound of water. They followed it and soon came to a trough of agitated liquid, among grotesque rock formations. They sat down on the stones, out of breath. Between the trees, amazingly far below, they could glimpse a fragment of the lake's sunlit gray.

A sudden movement drew their gazes back to the trough: it was a manatee, six yards long and blue, moving sinuously under the surface. How could it have reached those heights? There were hollows above the spring, and suddenly, from one of them, a large tuna-like head emerged: another manatee, flaring its nostrils in the air, its flat eyes fixed on the movements of its fellow creature. The hikers refrained from all movement. They didn't know how dangerous those mammals might be.

Eventually, the one in the cave threw itself clumsily into the water. They could see its whole body as it fell: a female. They realized that they were, by chance, about to witness the act of mating. The male could barely control his excitement. When he swam upside down they saw two horns, one on either side of the anus, as long and thick as pencils, with sharp points. The female turned over: her anus was surrounded by bulbous rings of throbbing tissue. The creatures coupled and sank to the bottom. The water made their cries sound distant. They tumbled in ecstasy, still clamped together. A web of white threads spread out around them. When they let each other go, they rose to the surface with lightning speed and lifted their heads like a pair of swimmers, gasping violently: they had been submerged for no less than fifteen minutes. Then they paddled away joyfully up the river.

This left Hual's men in a dreamy state. They tested the water: it was icy, with an oddly clear and bitter tang. Perhaps it was the taste of the manatees.

They were so amazed that when they saw a human figure appear on top of the cave-riddled rock wall, they thought for a moment that it must be an unfamiliar animal … It was an Indian, the shiny resin covering his body tinted with a touch of rust red; his head was shaven and his genitals rested in a bowl of white porcelain held in place by ribbons. He was watching them, amused by the bewilderment he had caused.

"Good day," he said in a well-mannered voice. "Who are you?"

They told him.

"Would you like to come up and have a drink with us?"

"We'd be delighted ... But we don't know how to get up."

The stranger bent down to point out some steps carved into the stone. Once the others reached the top, he took them to a bench made of stone slabs on which his friends were sitting and playing dice. Perfect, painted individuals, with a relaxed and superior bearing. The women were holding long lit cigarettes.

"Are you planning to stay for a long time?" asked one of Hual's men.

The strangers didn't know.

"We've been here," they said with a sigh, "for more than a month, boring ourselves silly on these beaches. It won't be long before it's time for us to go; we hope not anyway—we can't wait."

"It doesn't seem boring."

"Not at first. But you'll see."

They lifted the egg-shaped dice-cups. They were playing with a magnificent set of ivory dice, on a double board.

Once the bets were placed, the little dice rolled, making a crisp and multiple noise. It was the only sound that hushed the birds. Empty bottles were scattered everywhere—it seemed that the players had been there for days on end. But there were still plenty of full bottles, and they proposed toast upon toast. Time slipped by imperceptibly. When the visitors saw how late it was, they had to say goodbye.

The prince, of course, was still asleep, but his men went out hunting for lunch anyway, and the children looked for nests to plunder. The sun had shone intermittently throughout the morning. Now it was hidden by a layer of light gray cloud, shedding pallor on the world. The best kind of light for hunting.

Once the men had drawn their tiny, toylike bows, they reacted to the slightest rustle in the foliage by releasing their pencil-size arrows with a convulsion of all their muscles. They didn't aim. It was hard for them to miss. The barbed bamboo shafts were so light they wobbled as they flew. Before long they had a good stock of various birds. There were many they couldn't even name, but in that region only the birds with white plumage were poisonous or indigestible. The Indian doctors knew how to extract drops from the little head of a certain bird, and these were used every now and then to hasten a succession or settle a disagreement. Cases of accidental poisoning were very rare, since one would have had to be very careless to eat an unfamiliar species. It could happen only at an overly abundant and entertaining lunch.

They carried the game on their backs in elastic string bags. When they could fit in no more birds and were bowed down by huge multicolored feathery bundles, they returned to the camp (they hadn't gone far).

The children went into the groves in search of nests. Climbing with monkey-like agility, they held their bodies away from the trunk, gripping it with hands and feet, which made them seem weightless. Apart from laughing, they were quiet. Sometimes a bird would come and sing dreamily over its plundered nest. And the child would be taken aback. Because of their eye color, the birds couldn't meet a human gaze, and the children had learned never to catch a wandering eye ... Some nests had a peculiar smell, which the children breathed in eagerly, an intimate and secret effluvium destined to return in dreams.

The booty was abundant: leverets, little frogs with fat thighs. Meanwhile, the women gathered wild fruits and tubers. Swimmers tore up water-lily rhizomes and collected the sweet bulbs from which the reeds sprang. Mint leaves were gathered, and small bitter gourds. They couldn't get enough, or enough variety.

Hual woke up in the course of the afternoon. He found it immensely difficult to come back to life after his narcotically assisted siestas. He wasn't painted, and the cotton strips hung loosely from his arms and legs. Before going out, he put on a visor of leaves. His eyelids were barely raised. The light, which he needed so badly to keep fear at bay, was painful to him.

He walked toward the water, deliberately inhaling the moist air laden with the scents of roasting meat and seasonings. It was just what he needed to wake up properly. His courtiers were hungry. They drank aperitifs and ate wild olives until the pigeons on the fire turned golden. Those late lunches were terribly tantalizing to the stomach.

At the prince's request, his favorite musician began to play a harp with three untuned strings, accompanied by a three-year-old girl with little bells. Sometimes the musician plucked the strings with his fingers, sometimes he rubbed or struck them with sticks; the knocking sounds startled Hual, and left him in a pensive mood. He ate less than anyone, nibbling at a pigeon breast and a few leaves of basil. But he emptied glass after glass of brandy. To the scolding of one of his wives, he replied that he would eat more at night.

"You might find this hard to believe," he added, "but I'm still sleepy; that's why I have no appetite."

"I don't find anything hard to believe any more," she said.

Fruit was brought. He took a sip of juice, between yawns. But he said that he didn't want to go back to sleep or he would be awake all night.

"Well," said a wife, "let's take a walk. You should see the scenery."

"Quite so."

The white glare was dimming so he removed his visor. He announced that he would go for a walk on the beach. He was accompanied by a few women and a horde of children who ran to the edge of the water, splashing each other and throwing stones into the lake. Seeing how happy they were, Hual felt like a guardian of youth.

A child found a shell with a curious shape and brought it to the prince, who examined it most attentively.

"It's odd. Is it a gift? Thank you. I'll use it as a cup."

The child's eyes opened wide in amazement.

"But it doesn't have a bottom!"

It was a kind of irregularly twisted cylinder.

"You're right," said Hual. "I hadn't noticed. In that case, perhaps it could be used as a whistle."

The little ones crowded around him, drinking in his words.

They brought him everything they found, asking for explanations. The party came to a promontory, which interrupted the beach. Hual didn't want to go any further. The children climbed the outcrop and leaped into the water, shrieking and making a terrific racket. Then they returned, in no hurry. The day was strange; it was getting dark for no reason, as if the clouds were growing denser without moving. There were no birds. The sounds coming over the water were ghostly.

The group dispersed again, but this time no one went far: just into the undergrowth or down to the water's edge. The prince asked for more music.

"I need it," he said, "to regain the sense of my life's asymmetry."

How exhausting it was just to take a few steps! Tomorrow without fail he would start exercising. But how? Horseback riding seemed awkward, and hunting with a bow and arrows bored him. Swimming, maybe. He had been a big swimmer in his adolescence.

He sat down on the grass and looked at the lake. The surface of the water seemed taut for some mysterious reason; there was something hidden beneath it, producing a delicious suspense.

"That's how it is," thought Hual. "Many things lie hidden underwater: the sublime forms of beauty, which I cannot even imagine. And the worst of it is that now, right now, they are being made and unmade. Everything is irretrievable. And beauty always dissolves before it is seen."

Then it occurred to him that perhaps there was nothing under the water.

"But in that case water itself is elegance in its supreme degree. It is a sunken galleon."

The prince turned his gaze to the women and warriors nearby. Most were asleep, but a few were smoking or drinking, lying back looking at the clouds, playing dice or talking quietly.

His eye lingered on a young white woman, the newest of his half wives, who had been with him no more than a few weeks. She was nursing a naked little girl, two or three months old. She didn't look European and was barely different from the Indian women sitting around her. He couldn't remember who had told him that she was white. Some fragments of her history had reached his royal ears.

Dodi, a powerful chief from the south, had taken a fancy to this woman and bought her from the men who had captured her in a raid on some obscure fort. To dispel her sadness, he had moved heaven and earth to find the son from whom she had been separated. And yet the marriage had ended almost immediately. Perhaps Dodi had ceased to love her when she ceased to be sad. Had they parted on good terms? She appeared at Hual's court soon afterward, and they asked her no questions. The prince thought her pretty: fragile and small, with delicate hands.

She was as absorbed as her baby daughter in the feeding. Beside her, another young woman was feeding a newborn baby girl with the same concentration ... Hual was disconcerted. The two mothers were so alike, he couldn't be sure he hadn't mixed them up.

The light was failing. The days were not yet very long, but the savages behaved as if they were. Those who were waking up from their siestas went for a swim. They walked out into the still white water. It began to drizzle. The prince took refuge under an awning of waxed paper and called for drinks and cigars. His mind was a blank. He watched the swimmers, some of whom were very far from the shore. He felt certain vague anxieties. A mysterious desire.

Suddenly he heard them all cry out and start swimming toward a point where there was a stirring in the water. They appeared to have found some aquatic creature and to be trying to catch it. Hual thought it might be a giant tortoise. The swimmers were about a hundred yards from the shore, but the water wasn't deep; it came up only to their chests. The creature, whatever it was, must have been very large and vigorous. Everyone was shouting, jumping, and splashing.

Finally they lifted the creature out of the water, and Hual could see it: a fish as big as a man, an enormous finless cylinder, two yards long, and white or faintly pink. The copper-colored bodies holding it seemed to be clasping a very white woman. With great difficulty, the men began to transport it toward the shore. Every time it wriggled, they were plunged underwater or lost their grip. Nevertheless, they managed to get the fish up onto the beach and toss it on the sand, well away from the water's edge.

In spite of the drizzle, Hual came out from under the awning, holding his cup, and drew near. The fish was dying with its eyes open. Its skin had a superlative smoothness and sheen. The children bent down to touch it. They were all saddened by the death of such a beautiful creature. Hual was in a philosophical mood.

"Life," he said, "is a primitive phenomenon, destined to vanish entirely. But extinction is not and will not be sudden. If it were, we would not be here. Destiny is what gives the incomplete and the open their aesthetic force. Then it retires to the sky. Destiny is a grand retiree. It has nothing to do with the human body's anxious perceiving, which is more kinesthetic than visual, or in any case more imaginary than real. Destiny is concerned only with the flower, but the flower has no weight; we want the melon. The melon flower is like a little yellow-brown orchid. The vines of the melon spread over the ground chaotically, in a way that is not lifelike at all. We're interested in things that have solidity and give, things that take up space, not conversations!"

A pause.

"This creature, is it not an apparition? It makes me think of the insignificance of life, how excessive it is, too full of things and thereby liable to ridicule. But thought is not overelaborate. It's all a question of periods and moments of anticipation, and human life with all its drama is no more than a part of the moment."

His men were listening in reverent silence.

"And this moment, born of melancholy, what is it but a portrait of the human race? Everything is strange; everything is impossible. For example, the fact that we are gathered here looking at a fish. Our faculties are scattered, wandering the world in search of beauty; but the fish has forgotten evolution."

At that moment, as if intending to prove him wrong, the fish wriggled and spat out a mouthful of pearly water, then lay still again. Hual continued:

"An event is always the inverted image of what does not occur. Which is why one should not speak of existence as a homogenous category. I would say that all things belong to one of two classes, just two: scenes and people. Luckily we do not have to choose. How could we? Sometimes I favor scenes, after a copious lunch, for instance. On the other hand, when I consider the beauty of a moment, I sense the terrible moment of human beings drawing near."

Drops of rain had filled his cup. An umbrella had been opened over him as he spoke. The fish was dead, in its white and pink splendor. The prince's sadness was apparent. There was a gloomy tone to his stammering. When he lifted the cup to his lips, he discovered that his liquor had been diluted and he poured it away. He was already on his way back to the awning when inspiration struck: he would take the fish and give it to Islaí as a gift, straight away; they would eat it for dinner.

It was a superb opportunity, although not covered by protocol. But that didn't matter on the island. Islaí was one of his half brothers, chief and commander of several western tribes. On coming to Carhué and learning that he was there too, Hual had regretted that announcing one's visits was forbidden by etiquette, since Islaí was the only member of his family whom he liked. Now the appearance of such a wonderful gift gave him a perfect excuse to break with custom and surprise his half brother.

He had been told that Islaí was camped not far away, on the same side of the island. Soon it would be dark. As soon as the fish was loaded onto a cart (which his men built on the spot and hitched to two little horses), he gave the order to set off. They all set out in the rain and the dusk, accompanied by the cries of irritated birds. Disparate breezes were whipping up the water, and soon they were soaked. Those with elaborate body painting were sad to see their patterns running.

The fish gave off a faint pink phosphorescence. Lying inert on its bed of leaves, it was a rather sinister object. They preferred not to look at it. Someone spied the campfires ahead and spread the word. At the same time there was a whistling: Islaí's people had recognized them. Islaí in person came out to welcome the visitors, with page boys and parasols and paper lanterns. Hual dismounted and they hugged dramatically.

"I couldn't resist the temptation to come and have a little chat."

"I feel bad! I should have taken the first step, my dearest Hual."

"How are things?" asked the visitor.

"How are things?" replied the host.

They made their way to the tents, followed by Hual's retinue. Islaí's people were illuminated by the fire's deep yellow, which passed through the canopies and lit up the gauze of fine rain. As soon as the newcomers were under cover, they closed their parasols and hurriedly removed their bark capes. Their hosts lit more fires and bulked out the dinner with the provisions that had been brought as gifts. Soon they were all fraternizing. The visitors were thirsty, and the drink flowed.

Hual savored the contents of his cup without being able to tell what it was. Lotus cider. When he found out, he changed cups; he was wary of drinks made from flowers, believing that they diminished virility. But suddenly he tapped his forehead and clicked his fingers.

"I forgot! I brought you a gift."

He told two warriors to go and fetch it. Now Islaí seemed to be positively scandalized.

"You really shouldn't have! I should be giving *you* a gift!"

"It's nothing, just a silly little thing, something we found on the way, and since we were coming to visit ..." said Hual, smiling mischievously in anticipation.

Islaí and all his courtiers were speechless when the men carried in that smooth, pink corpse. Hual fell under its spell himself, when he took his eyes off their captivated faces. The bearers came forward into the lantern-light, the oily shine of their skin contrasting with the matte surface of the fish. The effect was due in part to an impression of awkwardness: a flexible, irregular cylinder of that size and weight is no easy thing to carry.

Once the charmed silence was broken, everyone blurted out exclamations and comments.

"It's a mullet!" a fisherman claimed authoritatively.

"It's a queen manatee!" said another.

Unconsciously, they were reaching for feminine names, because the creature looked so much like a white woman at first glance. And the first thing Islaí said was:

"I thought you had brought me a dead captive woman."

"I'm sure that would have pleased you more."

"Not at all! I've been given hundreds of captive women, but this …"

He couldn't find the words. He told his people to clean and roast the fish. But first, he had two of his most skilled butchers peel off the skin, which they did in two minutes, in front of everyone. It was fascinating to watch them at work. What they removed turned out to be a very heavy, soft silk of the most exquisite pink. Islaí couldn't help noticing the look of envy and sorrow that appeared on Hual's face and, on a generous impulse, offered to share this treasure with him. Undeterred by Hual's lukewarm protests, he had it cut in half there and then.

"I accept it," said Hual. "I'll have it made into a waistcoat."

"And I'll have my half made into a set of belts."

In their excitement they drank like seals, and everyone imitated them. The creature was pierced lengthways with a spit, and promptly roasted. The chiefs were served first. The flesh was delicate but insipid, in spite of which Islaí pronounced all the words of praise that came into his mouth and rolled his eyes as he chewed. Then they ate snails.

Islaí was a great music lover (and composer). He never went anywhere without a complete orchestra of triangles, bells, drumsticks, harps, and all kinds of instruments, some of which he had designed or adapted himself. He had trumpets two yards long, for instance, which produced an indescribably high sound. But he liked to surround himself with discreet, imperceptible music. It continued all through the meal, but couldn't be heard over the conversation, and even when everyone was silent, the murmur of the rain was enough to drown out the concert.

EMA SPENT TWO YEARS AMONG THE INDIANS, TWO years of wandering or immobility, going from court to court, sometimes at the mercy of a minor king's whims, sometimes with a little band of young people, protected by the ambiguity of their allegiances, always on the move. It was, perhaps, the decisive phase of her adolescent education. She came to know the most characteristic feature of indigenous life: etiquette and license were in permanent, indissoluble contact. The etiquette of time, the license of eternity. Vision and rest. The sleepy sound of water. That was what they lived for.

Kings and subjects sustained one other in a condition of mutual ecstasy, with their presumptuous presences and the resulting amazement. Everything was profane, but daily life seemed to recede into the distance because of its gravity. They sacrificed everything for the privilege of keeping their lives unspoilt. They scorned work because it might lead to a result. Their politics was a collection of images. They knew they were human, but in a strange way. The individual was never human: art prevented that.

Their pastimes were smoking, drinking, and painting. Summer ripened the fruit of the uruku, from which they made body paint. Their designs were evanescent; a night of exposure to the dew or rubbing during coitus was enough to obliterate them.

The tongues spoken by the Indians were various but similar. With all the traveling around, the languages got mixed up. Apparently there was a dominant language for imperial diplomacy and commerce. But nobody was sure which one it was. According to legend, Pincén, the most powerful chief of the moment, spoke the "passive esperanto" of beggars.

The setting for Ema's odyssey was provided by the forest of Pillahuinco, which at that time extended for thousands of leagues to the west, sheltering the whole clan of savage cultures. The camps were set up in clearings, or out on the pampa: empty spaces, open-air observatories. Sometimes the band with which Ema was traveling would venture across treeless plains. The Indians who lived there were different, more unstable. The most remarkable of those tribes was that of chief Osorito, on the moor of Cuchillo-Có.

Ema spent no more than a fleeting springtime with Hual, much of it on the island of Carhué. It was a calm and convivial phase. Hual's life was a continual renewal of power. The highly prized black and scarlet varieties of uruku that grew like weeds on his land provided him with succulent profits. His social life was extremely intense: Ema had the opportunity to meet all the chiefs in Hual's orbit, who all paid taxes to one or another of Catriel's tributaries or satraps.

Although she was no different from the Indian women, with her dark skin and Asian features, she was categorized as white because of her history, and not just as a white woman but a captive: a romantic title that inflamed the savage imagination. The chiefs, however, were perfectly blasé: hundreds of captive women passed through their hands each year, and only a bizarre inventiveness could excite them. Still, there was a certain charm to the state of indifference, vague but not to be disdained.

After parting with Hual, she spent the whole summer traveling with a band of young people, the kind who took no account of time. They seemed to be living solely to prove that fixed moments do not exist. Nature closed its valves for them and presented a single continuous edge, firm and smooth: they called it "the gala edge."

Sometimes they happened on a specially curious place and spent weeks there, hunting in the surrounding area, or fishing, or collecting mushrooms. They fished using timbó poison and hunted birds with paralyzing smoke, which they released by shooting arrows through paper globes. Ema began and abandoned a collection of butterflies. She swapped her display cases for a little golden horse, which she named Anise. She had a saddle made with seats on either side for Francisco and her baby girl.

The group traveled on horseback or in lightweight carts, rarely going faster than a man on foot. Ema was amazed. They were crossing immense territories, and the speed of their progress seemed disproportionately slow. Yet they always reached their destination. Distances, she concluded, are in fact reducible to immediacy, and human movement is a transformation.

The first thing the travelers did on reaching a village was

to inquire into the hierarchy and make the visits required by protocol. They were welcomed with pleasure or, at worst, with indifference. When the time came to leave, some of the group might stay behind if they liked the feel of the place; conversely, a member of the local tribe might wrench himself away to join them.

With a few exceptions, all these people paid taxes to Catriel or to one of his subordinate chiefs. Some were richer or more important, surrounded by amenities and extravagance, while others went naked. But at bottom it was always the same: leisure and universal rivalry. They would often tell stories about the western kings. One claimed to have visited a royal court; another said that he had seen Cafulcurá's bodyguards, somewhere. Those legendary names set the travelers dreaming. Ema had conceived the desire to visit the home of a king, and she was told that it was not impossible. Since many of the others shared this aspiration, they hatched a plan to visit Catriel's settlement. They would have to march west, in a straight line, and the journey would take months. The chiefs they were visiting encouraged them in this enterprise. Catriel was, it seemed, going through a conciliatory phase. With the court "frozen," it would not be hard to get an introduction. Their hosts even gave them the names of certain functionaries and ladies (which they may well have invented).

One day at the beginning of autumn, the group set off at dawn, along a corridor of sunken flatlands, between distant edges of the forest.

They didn't travel quickly; everything was an excuse to stop. On average they spent one day in three resting and gathering provisions. But they were making progress. They could tell, because the places they were passing through were becoming more unfamiliar and strange. They caught and ate birds they had never tasted before, quail-doves, for example, which keep a clump of eggs hidden in their abdominal cavity. Occasionally some strange creature would come to watch them pass, intrigued. All the earthbound animals they saw had phenomenal tails.

They avoided the regular mail route because they didn't want to stop in the towns along the way, although they did chance upon some of them. One night they were traveling by the light of the moon (they had slept all afternoon), and they came to a village that was fast asleep. The horses made no sound at all as they passed through the dead streets. They didn't wake anyone and never found out who lived there.

Traveling south, their route brought them back to the course of the Pillahuinco, from which they had diverged a month before. They tried the water and found that it had a more bitter taste, perhaps because of the nodules of manganese protruding from the ground like giant cigars. The travelers spent a few days camped on a beach where all they could hear, faintly, now and then, was the song of a bird or the cry of a fox. Everything was familiar, and yet at the same time strange. The self-assurance of the Indians became a tremulous, indefinite feeling. Relying on guesswork, they supposed that the main settlement was not far away. Perhaps a few days' march. The season was definitely turning. The lizards were going underground to hibernate.

One day they came across a tapir, as big as a rhinoceros, with dirty, pepper-and-salt bristles all over, and two tusks as long as a man's arm. Its feet, tail and jaw were covered in mud. It stepped into the middle of the path, stood there watching them with an insect-like fixity, and made a snoring noise. When they threw a stone at it, the tapir ran away so flummoxed that it crashed into a tree.

But they hoped to see less inoffensive creatures. Catriel's gamekeepers, who excelled in the arts of husbandry, had populated his realm with the rarest and most beautiful species of pheasants, which in some cases were also the most ferocious. The first one they saw would be a sign that they were nearing the capital. Not the common charatas with their long green tails and shrill cries, or the yellow urus, but authentic pheasants with multicolored plumage and a hump.

And so it was. One day the travelers began to see pheasants. The first (the very first Ema had ever seen) was dark, with a fan-like crest and a disproportionate, smoky-black tail. It appeared on the forest trail and froze. The horses trembled and refused to take another step. The bird's beak was slightly open, and its wings shivered. At one point it shook its head as if to say no.

The presence of the pheasants ordained a peculiar kind of elegance. The long silhouette low to the ground, the wavering balance of the tail, the compact little head. And above all the cries, to which nothing in the forest can compare. The cry of the pheasant is the reverse of any music. A compact sound that reaches its full intensity with the first effort, or even before, as soon as it emerges into the world. Inevitably, it brings to mind the solidity of gold. One wonders how it is possible for the pheasant to remain afloat on the flimsy surface of the grass and not sink into the planet like a stone in water.

Further on, a red-and-blue shogun-pheasant stepped out in front of them. Just like the other one, it placed itself in the middle of the path and stared at them with a gaze that no eyelid had ever eclipsed.

Then came the turn of a big gray pheasant, one of the so-called Augustinian turkeys, accompanied by a diminutive parrot-pheasant, which seemed to be acting as its guide.

The day was a sequence of apparitions. Before dusk the travelers were lucky enough to see a golden pheasant, unexpectedly there before them. It shone in the shafts of sunlight filtering down through the leaves. Gazing at it for those few seconds, they felt the air darkening, the night coming on. It could have been a statue: an allegory of wealth.

Everything had fallen silent around them. Only the hesitant, faraway song of the goldfinch, and the thunder that generally accompanied the setting of the sun. The travelers felt that if the golden bird cried out it would destroy their eardrums. But it did not.

They had no desire to keep going. After eating a few leaves and smoking, they fell asleep. The next day, their progress was interrupted by pheasants standing still on the path, and then by something more extraordinary.

The group came out into a broad clearing that seemed empty at first, but immediately the colors of the pheasants, scattered in the grass, rose up from the ground. A whole flock. The dominant male and his regents, hens and chicks, all in the same mold: red, yellow and blue, slim like greyhounds, with puffy chests, delicate necks, and crests of shiny blue-black cartilage. They stared right through the intruders.

As the travelers had predicted, the following day they reached the place where the mighty Catriel installed his court each autumn. It was a low-lying site, sloping down to the Pillahuinco, with bridges across the river, jetties, each with its cluster of boats, curved beaches on both sides, and steep banks covered with bathing boxes. The travellers had an aerial view, and were captivated by the bright, motley jumble. A strip beside the river, roughly two leagues long, was entirely occupied by mansions, bigger and more beautiful than any Ema had ever seen. The morning breeze made the cloth walls billow, and the whole city looked like a rippling lake of colors: royal purple, blues, golds, and above all the Indians' emblematic color: faded orange. Here and there, in deliberate contrast to the silk and paper, funerary towers of white stone, in the middle of little graveled squares.

Not even the beautiful pheasants had prepared the newcomers for that scenographic display. They proceeded along the edge of the tableland for an hour without taking their eyes off the city below, until they found a descending path. They plunged into the foliage and immediately lost sight of the capital. There were tents or little makeshift shelters among the plants, which must have been the rest houses of functionaries.

The group descended slowly, taking till midday to reach the suburbs. Inevitably, they stared at everything in a state of provincial amazement; everything was interesting. A veritable multitude was milling in the streets, people of different races and appearances. A riding instructor went by, followed by ten children on white mules. A strong, stocky Amazon riding a shaved goat. Two women painted like queens of the night: blue with white stars. A blind man painted black. Gloomy-looking fishermen heading for the river with rods on their shoulders. Carriages of bamboo and lacquered wood, which must have been occupied by rich notables, driven by servants wearing feathered golden helmets who used staffs with bells to clear the way. The children walked on stilts or swung on swings. Ema and her friends came out onto one of the avenues that led to the center. The stores were majestically large and very far apart. Often the entrance was at the far end of an atrium watched over by guards and dogs.

Hardly anyone noticed that they were foreigners, and those who did paid them scant attention. The city was invaded on a daily basis by diplomatic delegations sent constantly and for no reason at all by Catriel's tributaries, who numbered in the hundreds. The diplomats would present their respects to the appropriate official, who would politely direct them to elaborate lodgings on the river bank, where the buildings were hidden by vegetation and there was nothing to remind the visitors that they were in the middle of a city, except for pointed roofs appearing over the treetops, or the opening vaults of the palaces. Ema and her friends had lunch, swam, or went for walks along the riverbank, looking at the fishing boats, chatting with the bathers. In the depths of dark hollows, between walls of Spanish moss and white creepers never touched by the sun, there were secret little stores, from which a slow figure would occasionally emerge, or darting children. The vicinity of the river instilled a calm. In the afternoon invitations came for the individual members of the group, which then broke up definitively. Some went to see actors, others enrolled in the famous building school, most went to live with new friends. Ema and her two children went to the house of a warrior who had fallen in love with her at first sight, although he had two other wives. With him she spent a brief and tranquil season. He was a good-natured, boyish individual. His favorite pastime was hunting with paralyzing gases, and he was away almost all the time. When he returned, dramatically painted all over, he would play dice and drink with his friends all day. On one such occasion he told Ema that one of his guests, an official from the court, wanted to take her as a concubine. She was curious about life at the palace, and he let her choose whether to stay or go.

A carriage drawn by oxen was sent to fetch her the next day. She was taken to the royal palace, in one of whose wings lived the courtier, whose name (Ema never found out why) was Evaristo Hugo.

The palace's outbuildings and pavilions were scattered along the river; some were even built over it and on the other side. The complex was completely formless, and rather like a labyrinth since it always had to accommodate an indefinite number of residents from all levels of the hierarchy. The carriage in which Ema arrived entered via a side road, and when it came to a halt, somebody opened the door. Ema and the children had traveled with the shutters closed. They found themselves in a sloping garden, under a veranda made of raw planks, with white paper curtains. The minister, her new husband, came to greet her in person and showed her the rooms prepared for her according to his orders.

That was it. Her new life began with the absolute calm of an "always." During the first days she wondered why everything was so slow. It was etiquette, delaying the moments. Etiquette made them perfect, inserting perfect obstacles like clouds before each action, even the most immediate. And yet, at the same time, the obstacles precipitated the action, triggering it in a static reality. The function of etiquette was to make everything seem impossible and, more than that, to create a background of impossibility for all the trivialities and details.

Ema shared a pavilion with Evaristo Hugo's eight other concubines and about twenty children. The rooms changed shape from day to day, advancing into the garden and withdrawing each time the servants shifted the webs of rope and cane on which the walls of cloth or paper were stretched or hung, like sheets. The garden had the air of a miniature, which made it unique and much admired. Anyone walking in it felt like a gi-

ant: flowers the size of pinheads, tiny trees, paths too narrow
to set a foot on.

Close observation revealed that the garden was in fact made
up of two slopes, one above the other. The miniaturization was
an effect of the distance between them. The sound of the water
set up an echoing between the two lawns.

Every morning the women went down to the river, where
they spent the better part of the day. Pink rocks jutted out of the
bank; the children used them as diving platforms. The women
roasted chicken and fish, collected wild fruit, and led a mock
pastoral life. They were often accompanied by Evaristo Hugo
himself, or other officials. They would go out sailing, or rather
floating, letting the boats drift with the current around the dark
meanders. Fish were bred in tanks beside the river. On the
muddy little islands there grew a chrysanthemum whose flowers opened flush with the ground. Sometimes the tidal bore
brought sea anemones.

With the beginning of the cold came a change in the outward
forms. A vast weariness came over the men. There was a textile
fair, at which the women of the court bought caps and blankets.
Evaristo Hugo's wives ordered new rush mats and made quilts
filled with down. Herbalists set off with great pomp on expeditions to renew the medicinal supplies for winter. Society prepared itself to disappear for months on end.

Before the party to celebrate the beginning of winter, Evaristo Hugo took his large family to spend a week on one of the
islands, where he had his summer residence. The air had cooled

already. They traveled and arrived beneath an impressive layer of clouds. The first days on the island were melancholic, because of the gray afternoons and a general restlessness. Evaristo Hugo did practically nothing but sleep, or admire the fish caught by his cooks with a weary look on his face.

When she woke up one morning, Ema smelt the perfume of snow. Although it had barely dawned, the light was different, perfect. The patch of sky she could see through the window was of a blue so clear it seemed almost dark. A silhouette appeared on the paper curtain.

"Who's there?" she asked sleepily.

By way of an answer, a hand came in and tossed snow into the room, with a laugh. Ema was quick to lift the blanket, but an icy droplet fell on her face. She got up and went to join the others in the gallery; they were lost in mute admiration. The white island, the freezing air, the pallid sun powerless to warm the earth: that layer would not melt.

All the island's trees, blue pines and limes, looked like scoops of ice-cream. The smooth surface of the snow on the ground was an invitation to leave prints. The cry of the woodcocks sounded different, fearful perhaps.

"It's a sight worth seeing. Shall we wake him up?"

The minister didn't like to rise early. But he had slept all the previous afternoon, and all night too. It was just as well to interrupt his melancholy nightmares. He seemed at once delighted and sad, as always.

"What will become of the ants? Snug, deep in the earth. And the moths are larvae now, swaddled in mauve silk."

Evaristo Hugo sat down under a parasol—the glare was bothering him—and began to smoke. He fell asleep sitting there.

The children didn't wait for their breakfast, they were too impatient to go out and play. They held a snowman competition. They woke up the minister to choose the best and complained bitterly about each of his decisions. Then there was a snowball war, and they screamed so much that Evaristo Hugo decided to return to the capital immediately, before the children shattered his nerves.

The bulk of the family embarked on a ship with three sails made of woven rushes. Hugo left a good while later, with Ema and another young woman, on a skiff with a single square sail. There was a boatman at the helm. The three passengers sat watching the banks. It was all the same: a limitless white.

"What strange stuff snow is!" said Evaristo Hugo. "I wouldn't know how to define it. I think it's a kind of solid form, but not like the truly solid things it covers: rocks, tree trunks. It's a state, and yet we shall have to look at it for such a long a time ..."

He sank into his thoughts. As they approached the city they saw more and more children flying the white kites with which they welcomed the first snows. Evaristo Hugo smoked the cigarettes held for him by the women. The water seemed black in contrast with the land. Now and then a tree would move, for no apparent reason, shedding a snowball. The minister had decided, before leaving the island, to have a red square painted on his chest. Nevertheless he sighed melancholically. Ema took his hand.

"You must be wondering why I'm so downcast," he said.

"There's not always a reason."

"True. I'm weary like a beggar. I wonder when life will end."

The other wife laughed.

"I thought beggars led a carefree life."

"Not so," he said, shaking his head. "Before they can reach the door and ask for a glass of water, they have to gnaw at stones."

"Why do all the beggars here at the court try to arouse pity by saying they're asthmatic?"

"Who knows? I've never been able to work it out." Any display of knowledge was, Evaristo Hugo felt, a lapse of taste. "Look at that."

Along the rim of the riverbank, a row of black mice stood out clearly against the snow, all facing the water. Scared by the boat passing by, they opened surprising wings and took off. The two young women cried out in amazement.

"Bats," said Evaristo Hugo.

On the shore, a man on horseback was leading a flock of about a hundred lively little goats.

"The king's goats," said Evaristo. "They're taking them to the mountains for winter."

A bird fluttered over them, brushing their heads. The boatman at the helm raised a palm leaf and shook it to keep the bird away.

"The first white wagtail," said Evaristo Hugo. "They're so annoying. When are they going to exterminate them?"

Ema laughed at her husband's obstinate gloominess. He

was having an attack of fatalism. He felt that he was at death's door, a useless, broken man. He confused her. And himself: that was the only purpose that his intelligence served, he said. He told anyone who would listen that he had no understanding of public administration and performed his functions blindly. According to him, it was a miracle that he hadn't yet made a fatal blunder and ruined the empire's prosperity. He had a mid-ranking position: religious secretary.

"But after all," he said, "what is politics? Its science is laissez-faire. Its technique, the nose of a queen."

Or: "And yet politics exists. It is the speck of dust on which the rock of eternity rests."

If someone asked about his occupation: "My work consists of painting myself red and maintaining a sceptical attitude."

His motto: "I have a mighty hammer but cannot use it because the handle is red hot."

When they reached the city, enormous clouds rose over the horizon, announcing the continuation of the snow. It snowed that night and the following days. Ema amused herself inside, with some maps that Evaristo Hugo had promised her during the trip, and produced as soon as they returned. Each one, opened out, covered almost the whole floor of the little room to which she had retired to study them. Folded up, they fitted in a pocket. They were made of fine, wrinkly paper. Those maps would accompany Ema for many years, long after her departure from the indigenous kingdoms. They set her dreaming. They were painted with vegetable dyes applied with wadding. They represented Catriel's realm as the center of the world. Then the lands of his tributaries, the edge of the forest, and even the empty zone separating Pringles from Azul. The western kingdoms, by contrast, were barely sketched in. No two maps were the same, although many showed the same region. Beautiful miniatures stood in for absent inscriptions: the capital with its palaces and bridges, villages in remote clearings, and even the fort in Pringles and the settlement, where Ema was able to recognize the hut in which she had lived.

One of the maps, her favorite, was devoted to the pheasants: their distribution and populations. Meticulous drawings represented each of the breeds. The bigger the drawing, the more birds it stood for.

Weeks later, a page with white stripes on his face, a form of decoration reserved for servants of the royal family, brought Ema a message. Laughing, and beating elaborately around the bush, he finally explained that one of Catriel's concubines had conceived the desire to see her, and asked if she would be good enough to visit the royal lodgings the following morning. Ema agreed indifferently, although she was surprised. Neither Catriel nor his wives and children showed themselves to common mortals. Evaristo Hugo himself never approached the chief, even when officiating at a relatively high level in the rituals, and saw him barely once or twice a year, on predetermined occasions. But then she remembered something that she had once heard, the story of a beautiful captive woman, named F. C. Argentina, carried off to the most improbable of destinations: the royal harem. Until then she had considered it a legend, but it could well have been true. And that might explain it: the captive might have been curious to meet the minister's young wife, having discovered that she too was white.

The next day Ema was led to an empty room with only three walls: where the fourth should have been was an opening onto a snow garden. To the right, contrasting discreetly with this background of white light, was a gray, shadowy figure: the queen sitting on a rush mat with a child asleep beside her. She invited Ema to sit down on a square rug next to the mat. She was wearing a skirt of red cloth, and her chest was bare.

Ema waited quietly for F. C. to begin the conversation. When the queen spoke, with a shy puzzlement, the mystique of society life shone through. Her guest trembled and smiled. They had hit it off. F. C.'s imperturbable frivolity clothed everything she said in a linguistic precision that was not of this world. For Ema, it was like hearing Latin. Listening to F. C., getting a sense of her life, she felt that she was understanding melancholy for the first time. The Indians had dissolved the queen's childhood, falling upon her like the sky's most beautiful display; to her, they had been ideas. And now, after thinking by proxy for so long, imagining what was going on in those splendidly plumed heads, behind those magnificently painted faces, she had realized that they were not artists but art itself, the culmination of melancholic mania. Melancholy had taught them to walk, and sent them on a long journey, all the way to the end of a path. And there, with supreme courage, they had looked frivolity in the face and breathed it deep into their lungs.

AS TIME WENT BY, EMA WAS GRADUALLY OVERTAKEN BY an urgent desire whose futility exceeded all measures but the circumference of the universe itself: a desire to grasp the secret of the present, to penetrate the eternal unity of life and see the system's undulating veil, since in the world of the savages systems had the insubstantiality of the hummingbird's song and the iridescence of its plumage, while their manifestations were immutable as archetypes. There had to be a point at which reality, perfect incongruence, would get through to humankind. She asked Evaristo Hugo if she was on the right track.

The real, said the minister, was the State. And the supreme proof of that was the way it delegated its one inalienable function—the issuing of currency—to private individuals. Each citizen had a right to freedom, as long as that freedom was so complete as to exclude thinking.

"There's no point thinking," he said, "unless others are making it happen. Money is all the telepathy we need."

In the most secluded of the quiet clearings where the Indians practised their shadowy financial art—projecting the shadow of the human onto the inhuman—Ema saw their dreamy haste, a rush of inventions that anchored them in the world.

Everyone printed money; the means to do so were available

to all. It had always been thus, they declared, since prehistoric times. But prehistory was another simulacrum. After all, the economy cemented the Indians' only certitude: the impossibility of life. "Life is impossible," was the clearest and most definitive formulation of the idea—the model—and they kept it in mind at all times. Throughout their lives. Whether they were procreating, watching a cloud go by, eating a wing of guinea fowl, swimming, or waiting for sleep to come ... It was all they knew, all they had.

They paid with the bills they printed. They were constantly paying; they didn't mind or perhaps even notice. They were drawers, depicters, copyists, calligraphers; imagination gave them numbers, and the premonition of death. Melancholy, like an indifferent sphinx, proffered indeterminate figures, which grew voluminous in the sky. Life went on being impossible; the prehistoric aesthetic receded, like the Indians' education. Children learned to use the printing plates before they learned to smoke; old people breathing their last would rest their heads on ink rollers. And yet it was an activity whose secret eluded them. "Money is too much," they said, "and life is not enough."

Their secondary activities were genetics and pheasant-rearing. Ema was attracted to the world of the breeders, and soon began to see them, too, as shadows. As for the birds themselves, the luxurious pheasants that had seemed so solid and compact before, now she realized that they were shards scattered by a prodigious shattering of passion, and that their colors were signs of absent thoughts.

Thanks to Evaristo Hugo, she obtained permission to visit the gardens of the great. For months she went on excursions to fantastic, feathery Bomarzos but she found them too elaborate; their rococo lacked authentic strangeness. She wanted to go and live on one of the big breeding farms, the last sanctuaries of unreal work, hidden in the depths of the forest, well beyond the ambit of her usual walks.

Her husband, who noticed everything, understood the restlessness that had taken hold of Ema, and knew that her departure was inevitable. Without hesitation, in spite of the pain it caused him, he provided her with the warmest letters of recommendation for the breeders, and one day she set off, following a group that was returning to the imperial pheasant farm after having deposited its load of fattened birds on the sovereign's tables. Leaving the court, which she had imagined as a perilous leap, turned out to be so easy it was barely noticeable. Everything simply vanished, and within a few weeks she found that she had settled into different but similar surroundings. At the farm, the distractions blended into one another so smoothly that they disappeared. It came as no surprise to her that work did not exist there either. That was the last and definitive lesson remaining for her to learn. Then everything fell into silence. There was no anabasis.

Ema married one of the zoological engineers. Through the summer and the autumn she helped him with his daily tasks and went along to see the birds being released in the forest. It was a pleasant if uncertain time. She gave birth to her third child, another girl, so small and well formed that she looked like a doll.

Time passed. The world was filling with a deep mood of melancholy. The sameness of the days and even the blue of the sky, which had filled her with dreams before, now drove her mind out beyond her own life, into indeterminate regions. She felt herself vacillating, that indigenous feeling.

She told her husband that she had decided to return to the fort from which she had been captured years before. Together they examined the maps. She would have to travel more than two hundred leagues through the forest, but he thought it would be a smooth journey, imbued with all the slowness of the angels. He gave her two pheasants and two little gray horses, one with a double saddle for the older children. Ema would carry the baby on her back. And she left one morning, at dawn.

PRINGLES HAD NOT CHANGED MUCH. NEITHER THE AP-pearance of the village nor the routine of the fort had been substantially modified by the shipments of convicts sent to restore the population, diminished by raids and escapes, or by the arrival of new officers, fresh from the Academy and steeped in its syllabus, coming to fill the gaps left by promotions and disappearances. Espina was just the same, with his autocratic manner and his machinations, and so were the huts, which had been destroyed and built again a thousand times. There were still little herds of white ponies grazing on the hills; the children were as plentiful as ever; and the men persevered in distraction and vacancy.

The only discernible novelty was that now any settler who made a request would be granted a parcel of land, in accordance with a policy adopted by the military command six months earlier. This measure had been authorized by the government for years, but Espina had chosen to delay its application until he had created economic conditions that would render work absolutely unthinkable. Some soldiers asked to take their retirement, claimed land on the river plains, and constructed flimsy, lightweight houses that were destroyed by the first rains. Cut off from daily interactions, they had given free rein to their nameless desires for calm and immobility.

Ema lived on her own for a start, with the three little ones and two Indian women, in an abandoned hut on the edge of town. Then she accepted the invitation of an officer to join his harem in a mansion that he had built on the banks of the Pilla-huinco. Some months of rest and reflection followed. Her experiences in Indian territory made her mysterious to the men, who failed to connect this dark queen with the hesitant girl of three years before. Her imagination had matured along with her body. She took lovers again, but sentimental adventures could no longer occupy her entirely.

For some time she had been in thrall to an idea, pursuing its developments in every aspect of the landscape. Each thing she encountered became a part of this new system of thought. She wanted to establish a pheasant-breeding farm in Pringles, a farm that could supply the dining tables of the entire white population in the east, all the way to Buenos Aires. This meant thinking gigantically, well beyond what she could do on her own, because only a large-scale farm, like those she had visited during her captivity, would be viable. An extensive area of forest and fields would have to be transformed, which meant several years of work, founding a settlement, reorganizing daily life, occupying an ecosystem.

For a long time she devoted herself exclusively to visiting a wide range of Indian villages, never missing a chance to study the business opportunities or discuss them with the chiefs. She bought a few pheasants here and there, and eggs, and had some portable incubators built. Eventually she felt that the moment had come to act. She needed land—there was a site she had in mind—and a loan so that she could buy breeding stock of every variety. Through the officer with whom she was living, she requested an appointment with Espina.

The following day, in a meeting of slightly less than an hour, everything was settled. Twenty thousand hectares of forest and fields were granted to the young woman, along with a suitably generous loan. The sight of her entranced the commander: slim and elfin, with her oiled black hair, her Indian eyes fixed on the ground, and her beautiful dark hands. Her idea, proposed in a neutral tone, struck him as crazy. But he was aware that she had lived in the court of Catriel, and assumed that she had good contacts. If so, any business venture that she embarked upon, however disastrous, would serve his interests by widening the circulation of the money he was printing. So far, his success in that regard had been limited, and he didn't want to waste any opportunity to reach the great courts with his bills. Since Ema wanted to buy breeding stock, she would be dealing with the breeders, the savage nation's wealthiest and most mobile set.

The conditions of the loan could not have been more generous: half a percent interest every five years, the whole sum to be repaid within four centuries.

"By then," Espina said, laughing heartily, as if he had cracked a brilliant joke, "neither of us will be alive!"

As soon as the young woman left, he set to work designing the bills that he would have printed for her, and calculated how long it would take for the presses to turn out that much money.

They had agreed that the sum would be delivered progressively, as it was printed.

With the first installment, which she received two days later, she bought horses from the only dealer in town, a mestizo with devilish features, who lived in a shed with all his animals. He greeted her with a honey-dripping smile, and when he found out that she intended to buy two dozen horses, his eyes twinkled with greed. Right away, he began to spout ribald recommendations intended to confuse her, which Ema had to make an effort to block out. It was a long and irksome task. She preferred the smaller animals, typical Indian horses with little heads and big round haunches. Some were so shiny and compact they looked like bronze figures. Some of his horses were too fat, like barrels with thick legs that ended in snow-white hooves. Noticing her preference, the dealer promptly upped the prices of the animals concerned.

Next Ema bought a number of carts made of wood, bone and rattan, painted in loud colors, and ox teams to pull them.

Finally, she decided to select at least a part of the staff who would be working under her orders. White people were out of the question, so she would search among the Indians. Many of the young people would appreciate the change. Early one morning she went to the beach where they had breakfast, accompanied by one of the girls who looked after her children.

As soon as Ema arrived, the Indians said to her: "There's Bob Ignaze."

The dawn light was still uncertain. She looked at the figures emerging from the water and recognized Ignaze, a famous dandy, an adolescent Tarzan. She hadn't thought of him, but there was nothing to be lost by offering him the job. Ema approached the circle in which he was standing and waited for him to finish off a pail of milk. He lived almost exclusively on milk and the blood of birds. She took him aside and explained what it was about.

"Why me?" asked Bob.

Ema shrugged her shoulders.

"Why not?"

Thoughtfully, the young man half closed his eyes.

"Pheasants?" he repeated, as if he hadn't understood.

She explained briefly where the farm would be and gave him a rough summary of her ideas about how to manage such an operation. They were sitting on the grass, smoking.

"Delighted to accept. I was waiting for something like this."

He leaped to his feet and grabbed the arm of a young man who had just come out of the water, dripping wet.

"This is my cousin Iván," he said to Ema. "Will you come with us?"

"Of course," said Iván in a sleepy voice. He seemed to think that he was being invited to go for a walk.

There was more light now, and Ema could see them clearly. Both had their faces painted black down to the base of the nose. That was what gave them an animal appearance. In the midst of that thick black paint, under eyelids heavy as moss, their small, squinting eyes shone cruel and birdlike.

"Who else?" said Bob, looking around.

He pointed to a circle of Indian men and women.

"They're all trustworthy."

He went over to speak with them. A moment later he brought back a man with painted arms, who thanked Ema for having thought of him and his comrades. His only condition was that they should be allowed to bring their girlfriends. Ema did not object to that. She spent the rest of the morning speaking with about twenty young Indian men. Some had not yet received a genital covering. They were accompanied by their fiancées or girlfriends, many of whom had babies or were pregnant. The first group of rearers would number about fifty, by Ema's estimate.

The rendezvous was arranged for the end of that afternoon, on the road leading west, at the edge of the village. Ema told the Indians to go to the horse dealer's shed to collect the animals. Since Bob had nothing to do, he went with her to the store to buy building materials. Throughout the proceedings he displayed indifference and disdain. Operating autonomously, the Indians couldn't understand why anyone would buy things in a store, when nature provided everything for free. This struck Ema as a moral question and she was sure that one day someone would point to this difference in order to vaunt the superiority of white people over Indians. Whites agreed to pay for everything, and that created a background in which things were free of charge, which is what made Indians Indians.

Ema left the loaded carts and went to her lodgings. Since she had time, she washed the children, combed their hair, put their things into a bag and said goodbye to the officer and his wives, inviting them to visit her some time.

"If it doesn't work out with the birds," said her husband, "come back to us."

"Goodbye."

The sun was setting as she left the village on her little gray horse, riding sidesaddle, followed by the carts. In one of them were the children and the Indian girls who looked after them; in another, the twenty-five pheasant cages and the metal boxes full of eggs. The pheasants, caged since the day before, were nervous. They screamed for no reason and some were even tearing out their feathers in a fury. None had touched their food, but they had drunk all their water. Ema had the upturned bottles in the cages refilled, and took the opportunity to add a few drops of a powerful tranquilizer to each one. Within a few minutes the pheasants were sleeping, or sitting down looking dazed.

The workers were waiting at the appointed place, with women and a considerable number of children (most of the parents were barely out of childhood themselves). They formed a ring around the pheasants, gazing at them in rapture. Painted for the occasion, they formed an impressive group. Bob stepped forward, unrecognizable under the black paint covering him from head to foot. On his shoulders, drippings in various tones of gray. His hair, shiny with oil, was tied up on top of his head.

"Let's go," said Ema. "There's no time to lose."

"Is your property very far away?"

She pointed to a place well within the forest, where the dreamy rays of the sun were lighting up the canopy.

"A few leagues. But at the rate the carts go, it will take us all night."

They climbed on board, settled the children on the bundles, and began the journey. Though short, it felt momentous, because they were going to settle in the new place. They weren't taking many things—they didn't have much to take. More than one of them, perhaps, was thinking that this pheasant-farming venture wouldn't last.

Before it got dark, the moon appeared, accompanied by the gloomy song of a horned owl. Then the stars, so big it seemed you could reach out and take hold of them. The children had fallen asleep; the adults followed suit. The women riding on the haunches of the horses rested their cheeks on the painted backs of their men and closed their eyes, breathing the mysterious scent of the uruku bush. Those who remained awake lit cigarettes and smoked them absently. Sometimes one horse would approach another, and a bottle would be passed from hand to hand. The night was warm, without the slightest breeze; insects and a few birds sang, sounding incurably languid.

They were traveling along the outer edge of the forest, sometimes close to a tributary stream, sometimes among islands of trees, from which, as the caravan went by, clouds of bats would rise and obscure the moon.

Suddenly, signs transformed by the darkness sprang up like rabbits before Ema's eyes, and she realized that she had reached the boundary of her land. She told Bob, who was nodding along beside her, and they worked out the time. Judging by the position of the stars, it could not have been much after midnight.

"At night, you travel more quickly," said Bob.

They entered the forest, heading for the river, and when they came to the bank, Ema said, "We can sleep for a few hours, until dawn. We'll choose the place for our settlement in the daylight."

They dismounted in the first clearing, a tiny circle of black trees. Set free, the horses and oxen began to nibble big leaves of wild chard, while the dogs sniffed the ground restlessly. Ema was feeling exhausted, so she took her mat well away from the fires and lay down, while the young people, who were wide awake, smoked and drank brandy without, it seemed, a care in the world. They were always at pains to seem carefree because it was more elegant. There were laughs and murmurs, and the paint on their bodies shone in the firelight. Ema let herself drift off to sleep, and when she woke, the first light was just creeping into the sky. Around her, the others were all asleep on their mats or slumped in the grass. She sat up and breathed in the moist, still tenebrous air.

She went to see the pheasants. They had not yet woken but some were convulsed by nightmares.

One of the Indian women woke up and stared at Ema as if she didn't recognize her. She had two circles tattooed on her cheeks, the eye-charms that were known as *omaruros*. Ema seemed to have the charms too, so neutral and indifferent was her gaze. One by one, the workers got up, and the first thing they did was light the fires again, to make coffee. The sky was taking on color; the birds were still asleep. The horses and oxen were lying on clumps of grass and snoring; rousing them would take some work. The trees' spore cases had been working all night like mills, and now the fire crackled as the drifting capsules fell into it and burst open. The Indians brushed their hair, and discussed the possibility of taking a swim.

After various cups of coffee and a cigarette, Ema asked the Indians who seemed most fully awake to come with her and choose the site. They set off at a gallop along the bank. With the sun at their backs, they crossed clearings and wooded zones, pastures and marshes. Ema preferred not to go too far: it made sense for her center of operations to be close to the village.

She suggested that they ford the river and return on the other side. Halfway back they found a low-lying area of about five hundred acres by the river, smooth and gently sloping, with walls of forest on three sides, bounded on the fourth by the Pillahunico and a beautiful beach. The ground was covered with clover, violets and wild pansies. Here and there a jacaranda, or a lime tree.

Air and sunlight for the chicks, plenty of water, and the orientation was right. The party dismounted on the beach. The absence of prints indicated that it was not a regular watering place for jaguars or peccaries. They didn't see alligators either. They discussed where the house should go. Some rode off to explore the surroundings. There were other clearings just nearby, forming an archipelago in the midst of the forest. They wouldn't find anything better, so they decided to settle here. They went to fetch the carts, which took a long time to cover the distance and, having laboriously forded the river, reached the site at midday.

After a quick lunch of roasted does and iguana tails, they began work on the buildings, in silence, moving fluently. All the materials that Ema had bought were used. The house was finished the next day, like a strange mollusc that had sprung up in the middle of the clearing. Six yards tall and irregularly shaped, with four rooms separated by curtains. The paper was light ocher, its natural color. Round windows with panes of mica. The Indians preferred to live outdoors, and it wouldn't occur to them to take shelter within its quivering walls until winter. By then they would have built other houses. Perhaps they would dig them out of the earth.

Meanwhile, they saw to the pens. When pheasants are subjected to an intensive breeding program, they need a lot of space in which to move around. The birds woke up in a frenzy. Ema had made sure that the cages were facing the forest, so that the pheasants wouldn't see people. Some way off, there were posts with little paper windmills to amuse them.

Toward dusk, when the cries of the birds were becoming unbearable, the pens were finally ready. They were just nets of string stretched from one stake to another. The pheasants tumbled dizzily from their upturned cages, falling beak-first onto the ground, which was covered with tender shoots. The two cocks were put into separate pens, with half of the hens in each.

The wailing didn't stop, but gradually the birds calmed down.

Looking at those twenty scrawny hens and the two wretched breeding cocks, Ema felt rather depressed. They were yellow pheasants, of the poorest quality, fit only for white people; Indians didn't even bother to breed them. She was just beginning to grasp the immensity of the task: to fill the vast forest with fine and rare pheasants, and make them a medium for wealth, as secure and convertible as gold. After casting an indifferent eye on the birds, her young helpers went to the river bank for an evening swim and a game of dice.

They were busy throughout the following days, setting up pens and even building a shed in which to perform tasks of which they had, as yet, no clear idea. They constructed big cages, a hundred yards long, raised on stilts, and individual pheasant houses with gates of sculpted gypsum. Hunting expeditions served to garner detailed knowledge of the spaces in which the future feathered population would range.

Ema sent her cleverest collaborators to make contact with the neighboring tribes and gather preliminary information. Each time, they asked the same question: Where could they find people who would sell them breeding cocks? That was how they discovered that one of the annual breeders' fairs was going to take place in less than a month's time, at a village not too far away (five or six days' march). Since she couldn't miss this opportunity, Ema sent a message to Espina asking him to hurry up and send her all the money he had printed so far. She began her preparations. Only her closest friends would go with her.

The commander wasted no time in responding to her urgent request: he turned up the next day in person, which was unheard of, since he hardly ever left the fort, and had never been known to make a personal visit. His interest in this business venture was becoming conspicuous. He brought a cart full of bills.

He arrived at midday, when the whole team of young workers was swimming in the river, and Ema was sleeping on the beach in the sun. She went to greet the colonel and invited him to step into the house. Espina pointed to his cart.

"I saw," said Ema, laughing. "Four oxen! Is it that heavy?"

Two strong pairs of white oxen were indeed yoked to the cart.

They went in. The colonel flopped down onto one of the rush mats. Girls came in to hold his cigarettes. Ema poured out two glasses of wine. She told him when and where the fair would be held, and said that she had decided to attend.

Espina sighed with half-closed eyes.

"As if you weren't aware that it's absolutely forbidden. But I suppose there's no other way to build up your breeding stock."

"No, there isn't."

He smoked for a moment in silence.

"And will that be enough?" he asked, referring to the wagon outside.

Ema's only reply was a "serious smile."

Sounds of laughter and splashing carried from the river. Someone came to announce that lunch was ready. Ema and the colonel went to sit on the grass, under some lime trees, far from the others. The meal consisted of woodcock and trout, and herbal brandy. Espina drank like a fish and ate like a tiger. The song of a kingfisher interrupted him for a moment, and must have made him feel nostalgic, because he began to tell Ema about the early days of the fort.

"When I arrived," he said, "there was nothing here, absolutely nothing. We built the fort years later; back then we lived under the trees, moving every night, never satisfied. As well as indigence, we had to endure the tortures of courtesy. The Indians looked down on us. We had to create a whole system of luxury to distance ourselves from the void. In that sense, my dear, it might be said that I was among the discoverers of the *horror vacui*. Then as now, the Indians thrived, with their obstinate vitality, while we were bored to death. Their supplies came through a chain of traders who were dealing with Baigorria. They received shipments of European liquor. We drank water." The mere thought of it made him sigh. "That was when I understood the importance of setting up a financial system. Until then I had thought that such a system could only be a form of sophistry or deception, one more way of complicating everything and humanizing destiny. But then I realized that it was a necessity: the animal essence of man." He struck a philosophical pose. "Life is an art: the art of staying alive. All the rest is trickery. But life is the ultimate trick, the only lie that can rise up against time. And here I am to prove it. You only have to look at me. I'm so old you could all be my grandchildren, but I'm protected by a great wall of scandals. Who else could boast so many?"

"What have scandals got to do with it?" asked Ema.

"Scandal is the superstructure of vice. And vice is the key to life. Life has no function, while vice is a function and nothing else, cut off from life. The only purposes life can have are dead. Vice has no limits. Vice is equivalent to knowledge. Vice," Espina added with a long dreamy sigh, "is immediate, limited, instantaneous, permanent. And there are so many vices! The longer I live and build up experience, the less I understand how the life of an individual can suffice to give an idea of how many vices there are. And yet it does ...

"And what is the link between vice and scandal, between the key to life and its most important manifestation? Money, magnificent, fabulous money, to which everything refers. And value, too. Value is an impalpable fluid, colored by all the iridescent oscillations of man's most curious propensity: to print.

"But I have strayed from my topic. I was telling you about the early days in Pringles. A strange time, which seemed eternal precisely because of its fleetingness. The monetary system was my obsession, and even before the fort was built I had an idea. I remembered what had happened in Canada in the early days of the colony: the governor signed playing cards and put them into circulation as paper money. I did the same. Luckily the soldiers had brought many packs of cards, and they lasted us a whole year." Espina burst out laughing and slapped his thigh noisily. "Oh yes! Good times! In my appetite for innovation, I went even further. I introduced a very special element: the joker. It could have any value that its owner chose to give it, without limits ... They all thought it would cause chaos, but I managed, with the help of despotic ambiguity. They all thought that having a joker would make you the owner of the world, but it turned people into timorous chickens. The new cards circulated. Nothing happened. The jokers were an unattractive denomination: no one wanted to hold onto them for longer than a day. They stopped you thinking. It was too easy. Now the other forty denominations have disappeared, but the jokers are still in circulation, although, of course, they have traveled far and wide, all over the Indian empire. You didn't see one there by chance?"

Ema shook her head.

"Back in those days, the Indians had good printing presses. They got them from the north, via Baigorria. They were always robbing the poor defenseless settlers. In the end we were forced to steal a machine from a minor chief just nearby, a certain Lubo. (Later on, he moved away, God knows where. Without a press, he felt emasculated.) We mounted a commando operation. It was one of those butterfly presses, with one bed for the plates, another for the paper, and a screw to press them together. There were two cork rollers to ink the plates. And a huge crank handle for feeding the paper. A clapped-out, prehistoric contraption, and the racket it made was horrendous, ha!" Espina imitated the juddering and laughed. Then he sighed. "But when the first bills came out, it was so exciting. I can almost see that sheet now: a dull gray, printed on one side only, with forty bills that we had to cut with scissors because we didn't even have a guillotine. One of the great moments of my life, perhaps the most important of all ..." And turning to face Ema, the colonel added: "Perhaps you'll feel the same way when you see your first batch of purebred pheasant chicks breaking out of their shells, shaking themselves, chirping, and starting to sing ..." He noticed the young woman smiling and changed the subject. "I don't know why I'm telling you these stories. Everything is different now; with the press that I've managed to set up we've reached a point where *there is no hard way* to get rich. Strange, isn't it?"

Ema thought about it. The colonel had the feeling that she would never find it strange. Neither that nor anything else. Could anything seem strange to her, the captive woman, in the midst of that edenic humanity, whether by day or by night? Smoking, eating pigeons, playing dice?

AN INDIAN HOLDING AN ENORMOUS POLE, SIX YARDS long, with a ball of feathers at each end, appeared at the top of an ilex tree, visible through an oval-shaped gap in the leaves. Birds and squirrels were constantly visiting the tree, but all eyes converged on the acrobat. In the sudden silence, the ting of a triangle rang out, prolonging the slight anxiety. The acrobat, an Indian of intermediate age, was so high up that he seemed no bigger than a doll to those below, with a shaved head and feet painted with lime, unadorned except for a broad strip of white paint around his waist like a cotton bellyband. He was gripping the pole in the middle and balancing imperceptibly. In the end, after lengthy preliminaries, during which the triangle kept ringing, he set off walking, apparently on air—in fact on a rope, invisible from below. With very quick, effeminate steps, he reached a place over the heads of the multitude, who were lunching in the open air, and stopped. Everyone clapped, and the tightrope walker resumed his quick walking, but at an angle of ninety degrees, drawing a murmur of alarmed surprise from the crowd. He headed off toward the gnarled top of a pine and disappeared into the mass of needles accompanied by applause.

Then the children appeared. They glided along those filaments—there must have been dozens of ropes between trees, forming a web—with a nonchalant grace, and some of them were so small that it was hard to see how they could have acquired that exacting skill. No one fell. An accident would have meant instant death, since they were performing at a considerable height. Some seemed to be much higher than others.

Tightrope walking, the only one of the traditional European circus arts that the Indians had also developed, was a response to the various levels of the forest. An Indian traveling through the Pillahuinco would often come to a boundary where the land began to slope away: everything was transformed and diminished, becoming part of a panorama. This was one of the experiences that had led the Indians to develop their superhuman conception of the world.

The superhuman condition entails a theatrical or pictorial gaze, the all-embracing gaze that gathers everything under one umbrella. That's why there are so many parasols in the iconography of the explorers, not because they are needed as shelter from the weak sun of the pampas, so watery it can be hard to discern the pallor of the light from that of the shadows. Likewise the parasol-hats in Darwin's sketches of the Indians, crude vignettes that always show them about to mount a skinny horse with a human face. Humanity is always the key to interaction with savage peoples: negating, verifying, or expanding the human, transporting it to a world where it does not belong, which is invariably the world of art. Anthropologists tend to get lost in a transparent labyrinth, not unlike the ropes of the aerialists, soaked in a shiny resin. That intricate web reflected only the scintillations of the atmosphere.

What exactly was it that they were suspending in the air?

The Indians were not always impressed by this art of walking on ropes. They accepted it indifferently. Occasionally a very fat man, like a sumo wrestler, would pass swiftly overhead, accompanied by laughter. Bad taste was always latent somewhere in their improvisations. Maybe everything they did had bad taste as its point of departure.

The function of the little orchestra that accompanied the tightrope walkers was, it seemed, to *stop* playing—it was continually falling silent. With those artists of suspense risking their necks overhead, there was always an opportunity to create a mysterious silence. According to the legends, the devil himself (whose name was one of the roots of the word Pillahuinco) had given the art of music to man. Not directly, but via a series of intermediate powers: the diabolical, art, the human ...

In the end, the sparse applause that greeted the first performances petered out, and the crowd went on eating, ignoring the show. High up in their leafy niches, the artists were also nibbling at leftovers. The marketplace was full of a motley crowd, sitting on the ground, or lying on blankets and saddlecloths. Chiefs of all ranks from a broad sector of the basin between Carhué and Bahía Blanca had turned up that morning for the annual pheasant fair.

The host was the chief Calvaiú. It was his turn that year to provide lodgings and preside over the breeders' general assembly. His engineers had worked for months preparing the showgrounds, which the visitors would tour in the mornings, and they had built an oval amphitheatre outside the village for the sales, which were the high point of the fair because of the bidding wars unleashed by the presentation of exceptional birds.

The most prominent guests were now having their lunch in a circle at the entrance to the apadana, while the rest were scattered around the marketplace. Hundreds of deer and game birds (including the white charatas that were a pest in the area) had been roasted. All the visitors ate their fill and kept knocking back Calvaiú's best spumante.

As always when the grand chiefs had a chance to get together, the topic of conversation that inspired them most was the art of printing money. And since they had all brought their finest work to the sale, there were ample opportunities to compare and note down new ideas. From time to time a murmuring commotion would agitate one of the groups, provoked perhaps by the sudden display of a very boldly designed or exceptionally well-printed bill. They spoke of inks, papers, watermarks, plates, and a thousand technical minutiae. At this stage in the development of indigenous civilization, the only way forward was to innovate within the system of paper money, so the ingenuity of the rich was always vigilant, always on the lookout for novelties. Each chief strove to protect his own "margin of originality," while doing all he could to intrude upon those of his rivals. They were constantly shifting those margins, pushing them out, as artists do, beyond the reach of thought above all, to make them untouchable.

Ema and two of her friends found themselves in the midst of the crowd, seated on an octagonal rug, along with one of Calvaiú's wives, who had been assigned to answer their questions.

The chief provided hostesses for all those who came intending to make a purchase, not just as a courtesy but also to ensure that they understood how the bidding worked and were able to spend as much as they had planned. Lunch was already coming to an end, and they were drinking and smoking. Bob had come to the fair with a network of black lines painted over all his body, and a black strap around his arm, into which he had tucked long red feathers. He was accompanied by his brother Héctor, an extremely thin young man, whose limbs were still smooth and childlike; there was not a touch of pigment anywhere on his body, but his whole head from the neck up, including his hair, which was cut into the shape of a helmet, was painted the brightest red. Not the opaque sealing-wax red of the uruku, but a vivid, metallic hue. The brothers ate voraciously while Ema spoke. They seemed to be less concerned than she was by the crowd massing all around them and the ambient buzzing of voices. Whenever the waiters went past, they had their earthenware bowls refilled with wine, brandy, or a white punch with an overpowering aroma.

Ema questioned her hostess about the origins of all the chiefs and delegates. She was curious to know what each of them might be able to bid.

"Some have brought infinite quantities of money," the Indian woman affirmed. "See that one sitting there beside my husband? He's the son of Mariano. He brought twilight bills of tiger- and tortoise-paper, stewed in a swamp."

All three turned to look at him. The dignitaries in a circle around Calvaiú maintained the perfect stillness appropriate to their rank.

"Beside him is Quequén, his cousin and brother-in-law. And next to him, a chief without a name."

She would have continued, but just then something caught the attention of everyone present. From the tent in which he had been sleeping, a burly Indian emerged, wearing the big headdress of a minister. The woman whispered to Ema that he was Catriel's emissary.

He was greeted with elaborate bows by Calvaiú. But no sooner had he taken a seat than he stood up again and came over to Ema. Everyone was watching him. He sat down next to her, averting his gaze and squinting horribly. They exchanged a pair of conventional greetings: they had known each other during the young woman's time at court. When the emissary returned to the chief's circle, Ema was examined with fresh interest.

"Who are those two over there?" she asked.

The young woman took a look and said: "Cayé-San and El-pián. Don't you know them?"

They were indeed the famous brothers, extravagantly painted and plumed, drinking, surrounded by women.

"Some of the birds they have brought are prizewinners."

"So they won't be buying?"

"On the contrary. Those who offer birds for sale are the biggest buyers, for the simple reason that they have unlimited credit. They're the only ones who can bid as high as they like without having to worry about paying in cash."

At that point, Ema heard a fragment of conversation behind her: "The longer I live," said a voice, "the more convinced I am that sex isn't everything."

She turned discreetly and saw that the speaker was a majestic middle-aged woman, with large tattoos on her face. She was smoking a long cigarette, surrounded by men. Perhaps she was a queen, although queens were rare. In the world of the savages, women generally renounced power, preferring the contemplative life. Ema looked inquisitively at her guide, who said: "It's Dedn, queen of the Aguaripayo."

Ema remembered the name. The little sentence that had drifted her way must have been ironic, because Dedn's sexual appetite was notoriously insatiable.

The orchestra struck up again, with its usual timing problems, to indicate that the toasts were beginning. Héctor and Bob had fallen asleep sitting up. They had eaten and drunk too much. But Ema and her hostess had their cups refilled and went on talking.

Not far away was a circle of beautiful Indian women laden with necklaces and covered with painting.

"They're Hebdoceo's servants."

Ema's hostess had apparently presumed that this name would be familiar to her, but since it was not, she explained: "He's a minor chief, with a tiny village somewhere, but they say he's the richest of all. He's the owner and discoverer of the Despeñadero sulfur mines and has one of the biggest breeding farms."

Ema spotted him among his serving women. He was a very light-skinned individual, wearing bejeweled garters.

"He's bound to bid strongly for the champions. This year's specimens are superb."

"I saw them," said Ema.

"And it won't be just Hebdoceo. Many others have their eyes on those birds. Especially Satellite ..."

This was the name pronounced most often in conversations all around the marketplace. Satellite was the grand champion of the golden breed, and according to those in the know, such a specimen had not been seen for many years. All the breeders were nursing the hope of outbidding the others that afternoon and taking him home.

"But no one has come from the western courts," said Ema thoughtfully.

"Of course not. The kings never send anyone to the fairs. They have other sources."

Ema looked at her hostess inquisitively.

"There are two ways of getting purebred specimens," she explained. "For us, there are these sales. It's a kind of craft: improving the breed by hybridization and cleaning up the gene pool. Buying and selling qualities and capacities. But the breeders in the west ..."

She paused, looking off into the distance, as they always did when referring, with the usual precautions, to the western courts, which none of them had ever visited.

"The breeders in the west ... the kings and the emperor ...

they get their pheasants from local sources. There's no craft or work out there. Or if there are such things, they're beyond imagining."

Ema understood. This was the mystery they were courting so assiduously. The fair itself was no more than a veiled and elaborate allusion to the great combinations of pheasants that took place in the far west.

Around the edge of the showgrounds was a row of kneeling horses. This was one of the new fashions, apparently; the Indians were inveterate dandies. Many had parrots on their shoulders. The musicians continued to modulate, but no one was listening any more. Ema had not gone unnoticed. More than one pair of dark eyes turned to examine her. It was rare for women to come as buyers. When the rumor that she was white began to spread, the interest in her intensified. The polite treatment that she had received from Catriel's disdainful emissary showed that she was well connected. They wanted to know more.

They saw her smoking with aplomb, and examined the young men accompanying her. Many chiefs made discreet inquiries. All they could find out was that she was new to breeding, and had the support of a white potentate, who, for his part, was new to the printing of money but full of imagination.

A minor chief named Pinedo, who was a relative of Caful, decided to go and greet her.

"Good day," he said. "Have you admired the pretty chicks?"

"I have," replied Ema evasively.

After a little more chatting, graced with a "serious smile,"

Pinedo went away. Then Calvaiú himself invited her to join his family group. Ema declined, saying that she would like to take a siesta.

"Did you enjoy our little music?"

By this time, lunch was over, and those who had eaten were under the irresistible sway of sleep. Diligently attended to, the Indians reclined on blankets or carpets to take a nap. Some went to lie down among the trees, kicking at the little horses to shoo them away. Meanwhile, the chief sent his assistants to check that everything was in order at the auction site.

An indefinite time elapsed. The sound of a little silver bell gradually woke them up. After some minor retouching of body paint and a cigarette, they were ready. They set off in long columns, unhurriedly. All the pheasants had been moved to the basement of the stadium, which had been built in a clearing two hundred yards from the village center. Ema was one of the last to go in. She had to pass through an archway, underneath the rows of seats, before emerging into the light. An oval field, surrounded by stands, which were already filling up with a noisy, impatient, brightly adorned crowd.

She looked around; the Indian woman was explaining something. The two pages kept their eyes on the ground, looking disdainful. They took their places in the front row.

At one end was the hatch from which the pheasants would emerge. At the other, a bamboo tower for the auctioneer. Bids were made by placing a roll of money on the little red desk in front of each seat.

Bob was holding the program that listed the champions and runners-up, with illustrations. That morning they had conducted a meticulous inspection of each specimen and filled the little booklet with marks. They were interested in almost all of the prizewinning birds.

From where they were sitting, they had a good view of the stadium. The chiefs and emissaries seemed to fall asleep as soon as they found their seats. They surrounded themselves with thick clouds of cigar smoke and feigned utter indifference to all the proceedings.

The field was covered with gray sand, stained especially to contrast with the colors of the pheasants. The birds began to parade straight away, and at the same time the auctioneer's strident voice rang out, spouting a superfast stream of words from his cardboard megaphone.

FIFTEEN DAYS LATER, HAVING RETURNED SAFE AND sound with her pheasants, Ema related her trip to Espina, concluding with these words: "I've never had to make so many choices in a single afternoon. But I wouldn't say that the afternoon was totally absurd. Meaninglessness was always on the point of breaking out, it seemed, but at the critical moment, nothing happened. Or rather, there was no critical moment. It was all repetition. It was exactly what people call 'a magical afternoon.' At times like that you feel that a scandal is about to rock the heavens. But for the Indians there's no such thing as a scandal. Because it's a human concept; it's the human par excellence."

"Although it does have an inhuman resonance," Espina broke in. "I've thought about a civilization entirely made up of scandals."

"By the time the last champions were auctioned, the light was failing, it was almost night. The stadium, which throughout the proceedings had resembled a basket hung among the clouds, now became an impluvium excavated in hell, lit only by the glowing sky over the silhouettes of the stands. The people sitting next to me, who had run out of rolls of money, took out catlike masks of jade. Some put on helmets. Most wore black sleeping masks without eyeholes. Everything had become frightening. I wonder now how I was able to stay calm; it was clear that we had gone too far. My two friends disappeared, and I had no news of them until the following day. They had been taken away by the priests. I kept thinking: Right now, their hearts are being torn out. I slept in one of the king's apadanas, a trapezoidal bark construction, painted blue. One of my frightening bedfellows gave me this."

With a nervous little laugh she handed him a golden ring. The colonel examined it intently, turning it between forefinger and thumb. Then he placed it on the ground. For a while he remained silent, with a look of concentration on his face. Finally he sighed and said: "I still can't understand how you managed to get out of there alive. I don't think any of my spies could have pulled that off. They must have been taken by surprise. But indifference is surprise in a higher degree." He remained thoughtful for a moment. "Sometimes I wonder if we'll ever understand the Indians. That limitless puerility. Among themselves, they take no pains to hide it. What can we do? We hide ourselves entirely, body and soul, but by adopting the posture of the aesthete, they can hide in their own presence. They're always visible. Like money ..."

Ema nodded.

"It's something I've only just come to understand, although I lived with them for two years. In everyday life, money, however powerful, is a mere instrument. But at the auction it revealed itself in all its divine and useless splendor. Seeing those rolls made me shiver. The marvelous veil of money that hides all things had clearly been pulled aside. The little masks are amulets. Their function must be to plug the gaps that open up in the operation."

"What did they do with them?"

"Nothing; they just displayed them. As I said, they brought them out right at the end, at dusk. The jade reflected the dimmest light, the blend of night and day."

"Money has always been a solvent. But quantity itself has a dissolving effect. Nature is dissolved by the quantity of species in the world. And the quantity of nature dissolves humanity. How could paper money, which is pure quantity, always about to multiply, be anything other than a cataclysm? In European civilization, sadism is the force that has limited transformations. The theater of money is an Indian invention. There is something contradictory about it, as with most of their systems: it's an indifferent sadism. For them, the sadistic complex has always been a social principle. Now they've reached a different stage in the evolution of representations. Sadism is power and pleasure; and, above all, repetition. They're beyond that, it seems to me, in the repetition of difference. They've reached the point where money simultaneously accumulates and annihilates itself. We're so far from that ..." Espina sighed again and concluded, "with our pheasant-breeding." Then his tone of voice changed. "Has the work begun already? Are the breeders producing results?"

Ema shrugged.

"It's too soon to be sure. The pheasants were sedated for the journey. We had to wait a few days for them to get over it, and some didn't acclimatize well: it's very humid here. But yes, the work has begun. The first step was to impregnate the hens, and they're already starting to lay."

"I'd like to take a look."

"Of course. We'll do a tour."

She had invited him to lunch, and they were alone in a room in Ema's mansion, sitting on mats, Indian style. Slanting paper served as wall and roof, and two screens placed at an angle separated them from a space in which some maids were eating. Between the two of them were various rows of plates and glasses, from which the colonel was busily serving himself.

Ema was holding the youngest of her four children, a baby girl, four months old. When she opened her dress to feed her, the colonel could not repress a little gasp of admiration at the sight of the young woman's breast. It was the image of purity. But he remembered the rumors about her that had reached his ears in the fort. Ema's youth was categorical proof of her innocence and wantonness. Lack of age was often enigmatic, thought Espina: it meant a lack of certainty. Although those children were an expression of desire.

An Indian woman came in with another dish of pigeons and left it next to the colonel. He made a mouthful of one, followed straight away by another. He picked them up by the claws, with both hands. He tore off the breast and thighs with one bite, chewed them slowly, and washed them down with liquor. There was a big round demijohn within his reach, from which he kept refilling his cup. He tossed the skeletons into a basket.

Ema waited until the baby girl fell asleep and put her to bed. Then she ate an egg. Espina congratulated her on the woodcocks.

"We've found plentiful game in this area," she said. "Woodcocks, quail, guinea fowl, lapwing. My workers hunt them for sport. They run them down. I'm worried that the pheasants might drive them away; they're so unfriendly. When we start releasing them, it will affect all the fauna in the area."

"When will that be?"

"By spring we'll have two thousand young pheasants ready for life in the wild."

The colonel whistled in admiration.

"That's impressive. What does it matter if those wretched fowl disappear. It would be a change for the good. What about the jaguars and the peccaries?"

"When pheasants occupy an area, all the big game disappears."

"I'm still surprised that you're intending to release them."

"Not all of them. Just enough to create a protective zone around the breeding farm. And we'll keep working on most of the birds here, using Indian techniques: insemination, incubation, fattening up. The wild birds will serve a different purpose."

Noticing that the colonel's attention had strayed, she stopped. A dish of strawberries was brought in and another bottle of champagne uncorked.

"To the pheasants!" said Espina, raising his glass.

He'd been obliged to undo his belt buckle, his abdomen was

so distended, and the effects of his fullness and the silence were combining to close his eyes. When Ema put a cigarette between his lips, he inhaled with delight. The smoke was very cool by the time it reached his lungs, and the pleasure was acute. The atmosphere surrounding them was created by Ema's perfect mastery of etiquette. They could hear the pheasants outside crying from time to time, and occasional bursts of laughter and exclamations from the young people, far away, and all these sounds were lapped by waves of deep silence. On the verge of sleep, the colonel thought that he could also hear notes made by an Indian harp, although he could not pick out the melody. Before his drowsy eyes the shadows arranged themselves into figures. A smiling cat with a geometrical head, a coiled snake, a monkey baring its teeth, which turned out to be white dice ...

When he woke up, Ema was lying asleep on the rush mat. The remains of lunch were radiant, transfigured: a glass, a silver saltcellar, or a drop of water on a piece of fruit gathered the light here and there. There was a plant in a pot, with almost black, palmlike leaves, fuzzed with white on the undersides, graciously curving toward the paper wall. Espina's movements woke the young woman, who smiled and apologized: "I fell asleep for a moment." She got up and went to look at her baby girl. "If you like, we could do it now, that tour I promised you."

"Nothing would please me more," said the colonel, filling a cup.

He was still drowsily slow. He stretched, stood up adjusting his clothes, and followed Ema out. The sky was still gray, as in the morning, but there was more light. It must have rained while they were having lunch, because the grass was wet.

Before them stretched the broad floodplain, sloping gently down to the river. Espina could see many Indians sitting or lying on the bank. The odd word or guffaw carried on the breeze.

Ema brought out two cups of steaming coffee, which they drank standing there. She was followed by Francisco, and the older girl, who had just begun to walk, carrying a naked doll with white shoes.

"Come with us," Emma said to the children, and they set off for the guided tour.

They went around the house. Behind it was an area of almost two hundred and fifty acres completely covered with breeding yards. It was surprising to see how much work had been done in such a short time, although the flimsiness of the constructions was evident on close inspection. It was all provisional, Ema explained. They changed the arrangement of the fences every day, according to their needs. A quick overview of the great labyrinth: rows of cages raised a yard and a half off the ground, globes of woven wire with little paper compartments, individual cages with parasols, open yards with trenches and drinking troughs, and sheds of thatched palm for tending to the birds in various ways.

"A glorious vision of industry!" exclaimed the colonel. He looked as if he were about to go on, but in the end all he said was: "Though perhaps a closer look will reveal the most glorious details."

First they came to the fence of a yard in which various birds were roaming free.

"What are they?" asked Espina.

"Female duskies."

"Duskies? Why are they called that?"

"It's the name of the breed. Didn't you know?"

The colonel was intrigued. He looked carefully at the pheasants, which were moving about in absolute silence. They were gray and looked faded. A very black down could be glimpsed beneath their feathers, hence the name. Ema explained that the breeders had worked long and hard to achieve that color.

"Gray," she said, "is the best, genetically."

She had bought breeding cocks of that variety in all shades of greenish- and bluish-black.

"They absorb a particular range of the sun's radiation," she said, "because of the dark plumage. And that gives the flesh a special taste. It's also why their eggs are red."

She pointed out the nests. From where they were standing they could see a magnificent scarlet egg.

"Why is it so hard for them to walk?"

"We inseminate them every day. I guess they're pretty sore."

Closer observation revealed that the pheasants could barely move: their legs were painfully twisted and their necks were stiff. The silence that had impressed Espina was an effect of grave debility, not elegance.

"Isn't it bad for them?"

"I don't think so. The egg-laying lasts a month; they'll survive. They have the rest of the year to recover. We keep them awake at night, and they lay two eggs a day without fail. That makes six hundred fertilized eggs, just for this variety."

The colonel looked up but said nothing.

They visited other yards, where the spectacle was similar. Ema explained as they went. There were a dozen hens of each color, walking unsteadily (but constantly), and almost all in a torpid state on the far side of pain.

"They don't look like pheasants," said the colonel.

Ema laughed: "Their sexual dimorphism is very marked. You'll recognize the males, when you see them. The females don't have the crest or the tail."

"They look like chickens."

They stopped in front of the yard where the Lady Amherst birds were kept: they were small creatures, fragile like porcelain, and their beaks, drained of calcium by laying two eggs a day, were translucent.

"We've had to give them stimulants to keep them moving."

"I was wondering why they bother to walk."

They had little feathers, like partridges. Mainly white, with the odd red, blue or yellow feather here and there, which gave them a messy appearance. Had they not seemed so moribund, the effect would have been comic.

"I like them anyhow," said the colonel.

"Their flesh is very highly prized."

They continued on their way. Espina stopped with an admiring exclamation in front of an elaborate semicircle of individual cages, each containing a nest on which a plump golden pheasant was sitting, too tired to lift an eyelid.

"We had to isolate them. They're cannibals."

"They look like they're about to die."

"They get exhausted. But they'll survive."

"I'd be sorry if they didn't. Each one is a work of art, a jewel."

Their uniform golden plumage shone softly in the afternoon light.

"Wait till you see the males."

"Where is the famous Satellite?"

"You'll see him soon."

"Is all the insemination done artificially?" the colonel asked.

"I wouldn't put it like that. Since we're dealing with birds and species developed in vitro, everything is artificial. But yes, we do the insemination manually. It's the only way to be sure, given their unpredictable impulses and the asymmetrical positioning of the cloaca. It would be absurd to let nature take its course with such unnatural creatures."

"I didn't think of nature for a moment when I was looking at those hens."

"Would you like to see how we do it?"

"Of course."

Ema took him to one of the sheds: a roof of palm-thatch supported by live banana palms. There were long tables, with cages, and instruments, and a number of Indians at work, seated on high benches. Ema and Espina approached the closest worker.

"The colonel," said Ema, "is curious to see the procedure."

"Why, of course. No trouble at all. As it happens, I was about to extract a few drops from this bird."

The Indian pointed to the cage beside him. Cramped inside was a superb Mongolian cock, whistling as he breathed. The colonel examined him. The bird's breast muscles bulged under the dark down. His eyes were hidden by a stiff crest.

"The first thing we do," the young man explained, "is to give them a sedative pill. I gave him one a while ago and I've been waiting for it to take effect. Let's see."

He inserted a pencil between the bars of the cage and poked the pheasant's neck. The bird just looked at him stupidly.

"Looks like he's out of action." He opened the cage and took him out. "Come on, we're only going to sully your honor, ha ha."

The pheasant offered no resistance. The Indian turned him over and parted the down, revealing a round testicle.

"How about that? Full already. We empty it every day at this time."

"You extract the semen every day?" asked Espina.

"We do. Purebred pheasants are very sensual creatures. Their livers have evolved to speed up sperm production. Now you'll see how easy it is to extract."

He inserted a very fine rubber tube into the incision at the base of the testicle and slowly pushed it in half an inch.

"Done. It will pump itself out now."

And, indeed, the tube began to fill with a white liquid, which flowed in pulses, and dripped into a transparent sphere the size of a die. It kept coming for a minute. Then the young man tugged the tube free and put the pheasant back in his cage. The bird's eyes had rolled back and his head was hanging limp as a rag.

"He looks dead," the colonel observed.

"Don't worry. It's the same every day. In a couple of hours he'll be up and about." The young man raised the sphere and examined it against the light. "Top quality. This would be enough to fertilize two thousand eggs, if we had enough hens. For the moment, all we do is divide it into drops, which is much simpler."

He opened a bottle and tipped little globules of sugar onto a tray, transferred the semen into a fine, curved dropper and put a drop on each globule until there was no liquid left. Then he counted the globules he had impregnated.

"Forty. That's a good stock. These little balls stop working after two days."

He put them into a bottle, which he sealed hermetically and labeled with a code.

"How do you use those beads?" asked the colonel. "I thought you worked with liquid."

"No," said Ema. "The liquid is very hard to handle. Come and see. They're inseminating some hens over there."

They approached another table. Working with the hens was much more difficult and spectacular, since they couldn't be drugged: the drop in blood pressure caused by the sedatives would have prevented fertilization. Four Indian men were handling eared and silver pheasants. In contrast to their docile husbands, the hens were struggling and pecking. The handlers were performing their task efficiently, but the marks on their arms bore witness to the fierce resistance of their patients.

They had to use their bare hands; gloves would have hindered the delicate manipulation.

They gathered round an Indian who was opening the cage of a silverish hen. Ignoring the shrieks and flapping, he tipped her over and placed her on the side of the table, with her head hanging over the edge. Her claws were opening and closing furiously.

"Hot for it, like a budgerigar," said the Indian, laughing.

He put his fingers on the cloaca to part the down. With great skill, he opened the vagina slightly and pointed to the uterus.

"Here's the oviduct."

It was a gristly white tube. He turned it inside out like a glove, revealing the Graafian follicles, which were continually giving off little ovules. It looked like the underside of a mushroom, pink and moist. To judge from the squirming, that part of the hen's anatomy was not designed to withstand exposure to the atmosphere. The worker proceeded more quickly now. With a pair of tweezers he deposited one of the globules between the gills; they saw it dissolve in a matter of seconds.

"That's it," he said.

He turned the oviduct back the right way and let the vagina clap shut, then righted the pheasant. Her eyes were bloodshot and her beak was trembling. She could no longer cry out and kept falling over in the cage.

The whole operation had lasted no more than a minute. Espina was pale and his knees were shaking.

"You don't think it's too cruel?" he said to Ema as they moved away.

"Everything is cruel," she said. "But what does it matter? It's hard to come to terms with animals. Let's go. I fear you didn't find our little workshop amusing."

"There was something wretched about that hen ..."

She took him by the arm, and they left the shed. The colonel was bathed in a cold sweat. They walked between yards and washing troughs, heading for the big pens situated on the hill, near the edge of the forest. Once the fresh air had restored Espina's composure, they resumed their conversation.

"How many chicks will you get altogether?"

"By the last day of the laying season, we'll have five thousand fertilized eggs."

"And you're planning to release two thousand? I can't see why. Wouldn't it be better to keep them all here, under control?"

"I thought you didn't like our system."

"Well, it's efficient, I give you that."

"My aim is to have forty thousand free-ranging pheasants. Starting with two thousand this spring."

"Why forty thousand?"

"It's a critical number. A population of that size creates what the pheasant breeders call a 'stupid ecology.' Then there will be no need for the manipulations that you found so wicked. What you saw is just the prehistory of the breeding program."

"And how long will it take you to reach that goal?"

"Four years. Maybe five."

"All those birds. You don't think it's too many?"

"Any less and it won't work. With that number there will be a natural world of pheasants. Which will have a double effect:

they'll cost us nothing, while for the buyers, they'll be exorbitantly expensive, like resources from some faraway place … Like moon rocks, for example."

Ema paused a moment to allow the colonel to digest this premise. Then she continued: "By that stage my property will be an ecosystem, like the Indian breeding-grounds, which are sources of infinite wealth, but so close to wealth itself that they become invisible, and give their owners the illusion that they are extremely poor, the poorest beings in the universe. You'll see."

They had reached the houses where the male pheasants lived, in strict separation. The architectural imagination of the young builders had surpassed itself with each new construction. Most were composed of a cigar-shaped minaret, leaning slightly to the west, and the pheasant house proper, of irregular shape, partly sunk into the ground. They were surrounded by loose laceworks of black wire. The remains of torn-apart birds and mice could be seen in front of the dark doorways.

"We feed them live prey," said Ema.

"But where are they?"

"They're very discreet. They don't like to be seen, especially if they suspect that they're serving as entertainment. But I think you'll be able to see a few. There's an Egyptian eating over there."

A male royal pheasant moving freely in the open is an unforgettable sight because of the disproportionate tail, as long as a sword, and the inconceivably tiny head. Whatever its rank in the hierarchy of breeds and families, a pheasant is always, in some sense, an apparition.

Espina watched the birds in silence. Absorbed in his own thoughts, he was oblivious to what his friend was saying. As they were passing a deserted ziggurat, an aggressive Colchian pheasant emerged from the opening. He walked up to the wire mesh and gave it a peck. A glossy creature, with deep red rectrices and a shining black bald patch. His eyes were protected by two flakes of dark mica.

"We've had to give him blinders," explained Ema. "The constant production of semen has weakened his retinas; the light hurts him."

"Now I've seen it all!" said Espina, laughing.

"But you still haven't seen our star ..."

"True, the famous Satellite! Where is he?"

Ema led him up a path of blue slabs to a pheasant house away from the rest, at the top of the hill. Its tower was taller than the others and leaning dangerously; the retreat was sunk quite deeply into the earth; and the surrounding area, fenced off with strips of cloth, was scattered with dusty carrion. Espina didn't see the bird at first, then mistook him for a rat. Satellite was tearing apart the rotten carcass of a starling. He justified expectations simply by being so strange. Contrasting sharply with the conventional image of the pheasant, he had no tail and his ribcage was so distended that it gave him the look of a hunchback. For a while, the colonel was lost for words.

"But he's not golden; he's gray!"

Ema laughed.

"That's what everyone says at first. Wait till he moves."

The bird shook himself, tugging at his prey. But it was only when he walked off unsteadily toward the drinking trough that the colonel realized: the color he had taken for gray was in fact the most secret shade of gold. Ema told him enthusiastically that Satellite's production had inseminated all of her fifty golden hens. Very few breeders, even among minor royalty, had a cock pheasant of such prowess.

The colonel stood at the fence for a long time staring at the bird.

"Come on," said Ema. "There's more."

She took Espina to the closest windrow, beyond which a steep slope fell away. At the bottom, in a meander of the river, were square pools, divided into submerged yards, with platforms and walkways. Everything that was needed for bathing the pheasants.

"The system," Ema explained, "is copied from English sheep baths. Pheasants and sheep seem utterly different at first glance, but they have the same aversion to water and they use the same tricks to avoid getting wet."

Espina and she went halfway down the slope and sat on rocks. They were completely absorbed by the spectacle unfolding at the bottom of the amphitheater. Ten Indian boys were diving in and catching the pheasants in the water, savagely plunging them under, engaging in clumsy amphibian combat, and splashing about tumultuously.

"But that's crazy!" exclaimed the colonel, laughing. "They'll kill them."

"Not at all," said Ema in a dreamy tone of voice. "Look carefully."

Then Espina observed the game in silence ... He felt as if he were gradually entering a dream or an otherworldly scene. The water made the workers and the struggling pheasants shine. The colonel felt a strange uneasiness growing within him, a disquiet, a sudden desire. This pheasant breeding was child's play, a game without consequences. It scared him. It was sodomy incarnate. One false step could lead to annihilation.

Espina was not so naive as to suppose that in one of the lives he might have led, he would have sat there gazing longingly at those naked kouroi. He knew that his personal Sodom was the sum of innumerable circumstances, which finally crystallized in the eternal instant at which his sex had been determined. But the same applied to reality itself: it was a scene produced by chance.

AROUND MIDWINTER THE FIRST CHICKS BEGAN TO hatch, and within a week the first contingent had taken up residence in the big rearing cages. Once established, the routine continued smoothly; so after months without a break, the workers could relax. Suddenly the young men realized just how exhausted they were. Indeed, they could barely articulate a word; every step seemed gigantic; the passage of time itself was a burden. They also noticed Ema's weariness; she was heavily pregnant, and looked drawn, with bags under her eyes. They couldn't understand how she kept going. It became clear that they all needed a vacation. And since the breeding farm could operate with a skeleton staff for the time being, there was nothing to prevent them having one, so they decided to go and relax in some picturesque location, at the most picturesque time of the year. The cold inclined them to inactivity.

The workers had no trouble convincing Ema. She had been entertaining such a plan for some time. The winter mood was conducive to reveries of elsewhere. A fine veil of tedium had fallen over daily life, perhaps because of the drop in stress. Travel was the most radical tonic: to go far away and let oneself sink into stone-like repose. Waking in the morning and hearing the cackle of a pheasant muffled by the snow, Ema was overtaken by restlessness. So when Bob Ignaze informed her of the feeling among his men, she nodded gracefully, and said: "I've been thinking and I already have a destination in mind. If everyone agrees, we can set off without delay."

"I'm guessing it's Carhué," said Bob, "that magnet for vacationers."

"Not at all. It's too far away. We can't afford to spend so much time traveling. There are other reasons too: the island is always busy, and we'd be better off somewhere quiet. The place I'm thinking of might have been specially designed for a month of sloth. I haven't been there yet, none of us have, so we'll be expanding our geographical knowledge. A site of historical importance, but its history will ensure that we have it to ourselves."

She paused to savor the suspense that she had created. Bob was looking at her bewildered.

"The caves of New Rome," she said.

The young man's face lit up.

"Perfect!" he exclaimed. "I should have thought of it myself."

"But will they be willing to go there? The stories about the mountain are sinister."

"Of course they will. Those legends don't matter."

Bob regarded himself as belonging to an enlightened minority, immune to superstition. His enthusiasm was unreserved. He went away to spread the good news at once. Within a few moments the famous caves, which none of them ever wondered about and many had never even heard of, were at the center of everyone's thoughts. Ema had studied all her maps. Their destination was two or three days' march away, to the south. The caves were the only trace of the colony of New Rome— a place of pilgrimage for the generations of Indians following the massacre—and were shrouded now in dubious lore. They opened onto the mountainsides overlooking Bahía Blanca so there were bound to be splendid views, and the sea air in mid-winter would be the ideal tonic for the workers, jaded as they were. One of them claimed to have visited the caves as a child and entertained the others with fabulous descriptions.

In total, they would be away from the farm for twenty days, after the next hatching at full moon. There was nothing to tie them down: the birds' rhythms were extremely slow; they took so long to react that it was irritating just to watch them. There was no need to distribute the food more than once a day, and there were no predators or insects to ward off. In the clean air, the pheasants were content simply to walk around the snowy yards, leaving trails of starlike tracks. It was all so simple: four or five workers left behind could take good care of the opera-tion. There were volunteers, who may have been frightened by the prospect of visiting the caves.

"What should we take?" the others wondered.

Their baggage was minimal: balls of uruku pigment, bow and arrows, herbs and paper for cigarettes, drinks, and a few small objects (ceramic vases, lanterns, etc.). As for the little horses, long inactive, fat as could be and brushed to a high luster, they were even more excited than their owners. They would have to go slowly for a start, since they were so out of shape. On the days leading up to the departure, they were taken out to run on the riverbank, and kept stopping after a few steps, puffing vehemently. Their bellies were round from all the oats and alfalfa, and from sleeping throughout the day.

"How could they get so fat?" asked some people, appalled. "I hope we don't meet anyone on the way. We'll be a laughing stock with these horses."

But others found the horses elegant, including Ema, who said that it was common to see horses that fat or even fatter at court.

A few days passed. The moon filled out, the eggs broke open in the incubators, and the little chicks emerged, red like drops of sealing wax, cheeping ceaselessly and eating all the grains they were given. It was what the workers had been waiting for; now they could go away. Meanwhile the snow had begun to fall.

They left the next day at dawn and traveled all morning without a word, unhurriedly, in a straight line, heading south. By midday they were already well beyond familiar territory. They were beginning to taste the flavor of openness and silence. Ema could taste it too. The snow falling on her parasol was purity. As so often in the past, freshness, the sense of renewal, was propelling her into an empty world.

The travelers stopped by the bank of an unfamiliar river to lunch on the birds they had bagged along the way. Where were they? The watercourse was not marked on their maps. They were leaving the Pillahuinco basin behind, so everything seemed different. After a siesta they set off again, heading south-east now, making a detour to avoid the mountains. Through-out the afternoon, which was longer than they expected, they proceeded in silence, drowsily. The horses were walking in their sleep. The group crossed broad white moors, where spar-rowhawks flew from time to time, under leaden clouds. When the light had dwindled to the faintest glow, they camped be-side another river, among natural stone fortifications. The first thing they did was remove the saddles from their mounts and quarter them in the shelter of the walls, where the horses fell asleep immediately. The humans, on the other hand, didn't feel sleepy at all: they swept the snow off the rocks and lit a fire to make coffee and tea. A hunting party set off into the darkness. It was simple to catch otters before the moon came out. A storm threatened but then failed to materialize. Gradually the night went by. From time to time slow flashes of lightning spanned the horizon. There were occasional falls of snow.

Shortly before dawn, there was an hour of silence and lev-ity which put them all to sleep. The first to wake rose quietly, mounted their horses bareback, and set off for a tour. They were intrigued by the region's fantastic landscape and wildlife. On a terrace not far away, they came across a fox: black as the devil, big as a calf, with a pointed muzzle, a tail like an ant-eater's, and the agility of a bird. They barely glimpsed it, in the dimness of that hour, as it fled erratically over the icy terraces.

The second day of the journey was more lively, broken up by episodes of hunting and the visiting of ruins. The travelers left the mountains behind and ventured onto an icy plain. The horses sank chest-deep into the snow. The trails they left were curious because of their big round bellies.

The group saw a water pheasant, which stood out very clearly. A flock of seagulls followed them for a while.

Night overtook them out in the open. The clouds grew thicker; darkness fell. They stopped where they were. There were some who said they could see the uplands, not far off. But to be sure, they had to wait for the moon to come out. There it was: the massive shadow. They were practically at the foot of the slope. They slept deeply, dead to the world.

The next morning, the travelers were so impatient that they skipped breakfast and made do with a cup of coffee.

As is often the case, the bluff turned out to be further away than it had seemed. But they were happy to travel a while longer. They wondered where the caves might be. The rock seemed uniform and solid. Were they hidden by the bushes? Had they fallen in?

One more step and they saw them, half way up: one mouth was round, the other heart-shaped. Two black, unobstructed openings, waiting for them up there, it seemed. The solitude was absolute.

Bob was walking his horse beside Ema's.

"So here we are," he said, "at the tragic caves. I never thought I'd get to see this mountain."

"It doesn't look very welcoming. How will we get up to the mouths?"

Bob pointed out winding paths carved into the rock, with stairs in some places. Ema looked at them dubiously.

"Will the horses be able to get up?"

"I'm afraid not. It's too steep and narrow."

A girl who was nearby said: "According to the legend, the ghost of Colonel Olivieri's horse goes in and out every night."

"Ghost horses must be more agile than these fat steeds of ours."

They contemplated the solitude.

"The whole place looks dead. Could it really be that no one ever comes here? At least it'll be peaceful."

"It must be very quiet up there."

Others seemed worried: they were wondering if there would be any game to hunt. They couldn't see a single bird.

"There's no place without game," said Bob. "There are goats and wild pigs all over the mountain. And on the other side is the ocean. The beach is covered with clams and crabs every morning, you'll see."

When they reached the foot of the mountain, they put the horses in a kind of ruined stone corral, and blocked off the entrance with tree trunks. There were some hibiscus trees growing inside, in places sheltered from the snow. They watched the horses nibble at them and fall asleep.

The steps were covered with snow, and beneath that, a treacherous gray ice, so they had to climb very slowly. Ema held onto Bob's arm. In spite of all the warnings, the children went racing ahead up the edge of the path, avoiding the steps. But when they reached the mouths of the caves, they didn't dare go in. The adults stopped as well, to catch their breath. They were three hundred feet up, on a big round balcony. They looked out over a broad, snow-covered plain. There was a dark strip on the horizon: the forest, interrupted by the blue profiles of the mountains. Down below: the horses, like gray toys. Deep cold and weightless air. No breeze. The travelers turned around. They were on the threshold, facing the darkness.

"Which one should we go into first?" asked Ema.

"The heart-shaped one seems more inviting."

"And that's why we'll start with the other one. It was the dungeon. Chances are we'll end up staying in the cave with the heart-shaped entrance, but it's worth having a look around."

They lit paper lamps, whose light was invisible outside, and ventured into the corridors holding hands. At first they could see nothing, but little by little their eyes became receptive to the insinuations of the dark. They noticed the ancient smell of mushrooms. The rocks were covered with all kinds of moss, thick as pillows in some places. For many, many years, the spiders had been spinning undisturbed; they watched the intruders with a placid surprise.

Further in, chained to the rock, were rusty fetters, once used by "King Bomba's officers" to quell the frequent uprisings in the colony. Heavy, superhuman.

The chambers were utterly dark. The visitors' lamps flickered, throwing out gleams that hovered near the roof. They thought they could see bloodstains.

Where the moss had fallen away, they saw drawings done

with sharp stones, hieroglyphics forming a halo around each set of fetters, where a prisoner had languished.

"I've heard," said Ema, "that the two caves are connected by tunnels."

"Of course. That was the key to the success of the mutiny. But we could spend days looking for the way through. It would be simpler to go back out and into the other one."

Which is what they did. The cave with the heart-shaped opening was much more spacious, less oppressive. A natural grotto, altered only by digging the tunnels and enlarging a portal here and there. The hollow mountain. It had been the abode of the wicked colonel and his wife, which explained the allegorical shape of the entrance. She had come out from Europe to marry him sight unseen, and on the night of the rebellion, her throat was cut along with his.

Here the tourists were subjected to a different set of impressions, less gruesomely romantic. They emerged from a straight tunnel into a large room more than twenty yards high. Light seeped in through the cracks and folds of the ceiling, making the lanterns superfluous. A still stone-light. Numerous openings led into other, smaller rooms.

Ema's party liked it. This was where they would stay, since they were near the exit but sheltered. The height of the ceiling and the invisible gaps in it allowed them to light a fire. The rock floor was warm; they could feel it through their mats. Perhaps the mountain was a volcano, with fire inside it. The wind could not be heard.

Their cigarette smoke was drawn up into the great dome.

It formed strange, fleeting figures as it rose. The children ran through the passageways, playing hide and seek. They listened to the breath of their friends with a tranquil compulsion. All the indications were that nothing would trouble the visitors' rest.

They roasted the partridges that they had caught at dawn; then almost everyone went to sleep. After a few hours, some set off to explore the passages, others played dice. And others fell asleep again.

Ema woke up half way through the afternoon. For a moment she didn't know where she was; she looked up at the vaults awash with a delicate white light until the images came back to her: the journey on those fat little horses, the caves suspended among the clouds.

The others were sitting around her, preparing tea. They told her that a snowstorm had begun outside. She was drinking a cup of tea when the explorers appeared, in a state of excitement. They had found the opening on the other side of the mountain, which looked out over the bay. This made everyone impatient to go and see for themselves. The children scurried off like mice in the direction indicated. The adults followed them.

They walked for ages along endless corridors. Since they hadn't brought lanterns, sometimes they had to make their way through the darkness, following the sound of footsteps. The floor remained level. Finally, at a bend, a pale light appeared, which grew in intensity with each successive chamber. The group came to a halt in a large rectangular room. The far wall was missing. In its place: a square so dazzling they could barely look at it. They stepped forward and froze, paralyzed by admiration.

The mountain came to an end, opened onto the void, at a greater height than the entrances on the north side. There was no parapet. But sitting on the ground, two yards from the edge, the visitors could see a landscape that none of them had ever dreamed of.

Nothing blocked their view. An immense, deserted beach, covered with white snow, and the sea in the distance, the famous bay, which now more than ever deserved its name: White. Everything was white: sky and earth. The snow was falling on the waves, which were distinguished only by their motion. Not a single bird traversed the air. The clouds formed a smooth film.

The group sighed, lost for words. The whiteness had shrunk their pupils down to the smallest aperture. They lit cigarettes, and stayed there until dusk, drowsing. When the cold began to bite they returned to the shelter of the inner rooms. With the whole labyrinth at their disposal, they scattered.

"Tomorrow we can go down to the sea," said Ema.

They all wanted to ride on the beaches they had glimpsed from the heights.

They played dice, drank and smoke, oblivious to the passing of time, until eventually sleep overtook them all.

At some point during the night (or perhaps the next morning, it was hard to tell), Ema woke up. She could feel the baby turning inside her. The fires were dying, and everyone around her was asleep. She got up and walked away along a passage chosen at random. The darkness was very dense in some stretches, but then it would be interrupted by the glow of a fire or its remains, near which, in a secluded chamber, someone was asleep. She heard muffled sighs, soundless laughter. She peered through an archway outlined with a reddish glow and saw a couple entwined on a mat. Next to them was a paper lamp the size of a die. They didn't see her and pursued their games, which sleep had probably interrupted a thousand times already.

Ema returned at a leisurely pace and took the route that led to the northern openings, where her party had entered the mountain. It was day; the sun had risen behind white clouds. Down in the corral, the little horses were moving. They raised their heads: they must have been feeling lonely.

In the afternoon, when the group went down to set off for the sea, they were greeted by cheerful neighing. They mounted the horses and rode around the mountain. Ema, who was approaching the sea for the first time in her life, sniffed the air voluptuously. They rode along the beach until it got dark. They went riding there each day after that, and even swam, protected by a double layer of fat.

One day, Ema and four or five friends set off for a ride. The horses trotted on the sand mixed with snow, puffing contentedly. After the morning snowfall the mist had lifted, revealing nothing but whiteness. The horses peered ahead with an anxious curiosity, as if attempting to discover new beings in the realm of the invisible. Then suddenly both humans and animals discerned shapes moving in the distance, white on white: horsemen. The strangers too must have seen figures approaching, because they retreated.

Ema and her friends kept advancing, and the others, no doubt thinking that it would be impolite to hide, now remained where they were: a few men, mounted on dripping horses that seemed to have just come out of the sea. They must have been bathing them. Covered with fat from head to toe, the men shone against the dull coats of the animals. Only at very close range could Ema and her friends see that the group was composed of five youths and an old man, whom Ema recognized as a minor southern chief, a friend of Colonel Espina. What he was doing there was a mystery. He recognized her too, and came to greet her with the customary formality, not looking her in the eyes.

"Are you surprised to see me here?"

"Why should I be surprised?"

"We're camped a league away, over there. I came out to exercise some colts."

There were all pure breds. The chief pointed to a white one, ridden by a boy with a squint and a fringe.

"That one drank sea water; he'll go crazy."

He burst out laughing. The youths were looking scornfully at Ema's fat little horses.

The chief invited her to come to his camp straight away, for a drink. He asked where Ema and her friends were staying. When he heard that they were in the caves of New Rome, he didn't say a word. Not for anything in the world would he have set foot in there.

The camp, which they reached after half an hour's journey at walking pace, consisted of nothing more than a few paper tents covered with snow, and about fifty men and women, all related to the chief. It was very close to the coast; more than once, the campers said, the tide had woken them at night. In the hours before dawn, they added, the seawater was milky and warm. They kept themselves covered with a thick, transparent fat, which they stored in a barrel. Each visitors was given a jarful. It was whale fat, so they were told.

They drank without respite. They played with feather dice and looked at illustrations. A compact gathering, full of secrets and sadism. The chief was hoarse. The talk was licentious. They asked about Ema's children and the breeding farm. She invited the chief to come and see it.

"Maybe one day I'll go," said the chief, "if I'm still alive, that is. Maybe one of these nights the tide will rise, and I will never wake again."

He was drunk. By the time Ema's party left, it was night. Just as they got back, a storm broke, and it lasted several days. They hunted armadillos and echidnas in the caves. They spent long hours asleep, and painted themselves with great care. They sat down to smoke in the room overlooking the bay, watching the waves whipped up by the storm, and thought or slept.

21 OCTOBER 1978

Author's note

GENTLE READER: UNLESS YOU ARE FROM PRINGLES AND belong to the Committee of the Signifier, as I for one am and do, it may not be obvious that back-cover copy never covered anyone's back.* But for some reason I find myself under the whimsical obligation to tell you how this historiola occurred to me. The setting is propitious to the sharing of confidences: a lovely spring morning in the Flores Pumper Nic, where I often come to think. Tomasito (aged two) is playing among the tables, which are crowded with kids cutting school. Leisure reigns; there is time to spare.

Some years ago I was very poor, and thanks to the good offices of a publisher friend, I was able to earn enough to pay my analyst and go on vacation by translating long novels of the variety known as "gothic": odysseys in which the female protagonists—sometimes English, sometimes Californian—transported the same old entanglements over hymenoptical

---

* This note originally appeared on the back cover of the Mondadori edition of *Ema, la cautiva.*

oceans, oceans of passionate tea. Naturally, I enjoyed those books, but over time I came to feel that there were too many passions, canceling each out like air freshener. No sooner had the thought occurred to me than I came up with the eminently sportive idea of writing a "simplified" gothic novel. Down to work. In the realm of the imagination, my decisions are swift. I resorted to the Eternal Return. I renounced Being, became Sei Shonagon, Scheherezade, plus the animals. The "anecdotes of destiny." For several weeks, I amused myself. I sweated a little. I laughed. And in the end it turned out that Ema, my miniature self, had created a new passion for me, the passion for which all others can be exchanged, as money is exchanged for all things: indifference. What more could I ask?

CÉSAR AIRA